Cam glanced inside and saw the woman he suspected was coming to mean a lot to him. As in love? Did he love Jenny? Enough to get involved with whatever was tearing her apart?

Yes, I think I do. Scrub that. I know I do. Somehow, when he'd been trying so hard to keep her at arm's length, she'd sneaked under the radar and stolen his heart.

To hell with it.

Striding into the kitchen, he gently removed the stirring spoon from her hand and took her in his arms. Then, without pausing to think about the consequences, he leaned down and captured her mouth with his.

She stood absolutely still, not returning the kiss, but neither did she withdraw.

On her lips he tasted wine and Jenny—a heady mix that zoomed straight down his body, switching on his manhood. Somehow he didn't think this was the time for bedroom activities. His kiss was about sealing his vow to look out for her, about showing he cared…

Dear Reader

Havelock is at the head of the Pelorus Sound in New Zealand's Marlborough Sounds, just twenty minutes down the road from where I live. It's known as the Green Mussel Capital of the World, for its locally grown mussels, and every year there is a mussel festival with bands, arts and crafts, and of course lots of mussels to eat. It is a vibrant small town and very focused on the sea.

When I was planning A FAMILY THIS CHRISTMAS Havelock seemed just the right place for Jenny and Cam to get together and work through their issues. Both of them have city backgrounds, and yet both find the lifestyle in this small place fits with what they want to give and receive in life. It's a perfect place to bring up two small boys struggling with the departure of their mum.

I hope you enjoy reading Jenny and Cam's story, and also enjoy learning about a little treasure at the top of the South Island.

I'd love to hear from you on sue.mackay56@yahoo.com

You can also drop by www.suemackay.co.nz to catch up on my latest releases and get a copy of the recipe of the month.

Cheers!

Sue

A FAMILY
THIS CHRISTMAS

BY
SUE MacKAY

First published in Great Britain 2014
by Mills & Boon, an imprint of Harlequin (UK) Limited,
Large Print edition 2015
Eton House, 18-24 Paradise Road,
Richmond, Surrey, TW9 1SR

© 2014 Sue MacKay

ISBN: 978-0-263-25483-9

Harlequin (UK) Limited's policy is to use papers that are natural, renewable and recyclable products and made from wood grown in sustainable forests. The logging and manufacturing processes conform to the legal environmental regulations of the country of origin.

Printed and bound in Great Britain
by CPI Antony Rowe, Chippenham, Wiltshire

With a background of working in medical laboratories and a love of the romance genre, it is no surprise that **Sue MacKay** writes Mills & Boon® Medical Romance™ stories. An avid reader all her life, she wrote her first story at age eight—about a prince, of course. She lives with her own hero in the beautiful Marlborough Sounds, at the top of New Zealand's South Island, where she indulges her passions for the outdoors, the sea and cycling.

Recent titles by Sue MacKay:

THE MIDWIFE'S SON
A FATHER FOR HER BABY
FROM DUTY TO DADDY
THE GIFT OF A CHILD
YOU, ME AND A FAMILY
CHRISTMAS WITH DR DELICIOUS
EVERY BOY'S DREAM DAD
THE DANGERS OF DATING YOUR BOSS
SURGEON IN A WEDDING DRESS
RETURN OF THE MAVERICK
PLAYBOY DOCTOR TO DOTING DAD
THEIR MARRIAGE MIRACLE

These books are also available in eBook format from www.millsandboon.co.uk

CHAPTER ONE

'WATCH OUT!' THE SHOUT was followed by something like a muffled scream ricocheting through the air, lifting the hairs on the back of Cameron Roberts's neck.

Then the clattering sound of what Cam swore was one of the twins' skateboards hitting the pavement the wrong way up. His gut tightened, and his heart squeezed. What now? Was there no end to the trouble his boys could get into? They were only eight yet could kick up more messy problems than a team of rugby players out on the town after a hard game.

Already moving towards the front of his house, he dropped the hedge trimmer on the barbecue table on the way past. 'Marcus? Andrew? You guys okay?'

'Dad, hurry. She needs a doctor. I didn't mean it. I promise. I'm sorry.' Marcus appeared at the end of their drive, tears streaming down his worried little face.

Cam's gut became a knot. What had Marcus done this time? And where was Andrew? Had something happened to him? That would explain the fear in Marcus's cry. Except he'd said *she* needed a doctor. 'What's happened?' He ruffled Marcus's hair on the way past, begging the parenting gods to give him a break for once.

As usual those particular gods were on holiday if the sight before him was anything to go by. 'One day, just one whole, disaster-free day, is all I ask for,' he muttered under his breath as he reached the redhead lying in an awkward bundle on the pavement.

Her face was contorted in agony and the eyes she raised to him were darkened with that pain. Judging by the rapid rise and fall of her chest, her resp rate was raised. Blood smeared across her left elbow and down her arm, probably from scraping along the concrete.

Andrew stood, hopping from one foot to the other, his skateboard dangling from his hand as he stared down at the woman as though he couldn't understand how she'd got there. A second skateboard lay upside down beside her. Marcus's.

'What happened?' Cam repeated, as he dropped to his knees beside the woman. Swearing was forbidden in their house, and that went for out on the pavement too, but Cam came very close to breaking that rule right at this moment.

'Dad, the lady's hurt, but—'

'We didn't mean it. True.' The wobble in Andrew's voice as he finished Marcus's sentence told Cam heaps.

The woman moved, groaned. 'My ankle's broken.'

Glancing down her leg, he noted one foot and ankle already swelling. Fracture or sprain? 'We don't know that for sure yet.'

'I do.' She sounded very certain. Not to mention angry.

Guess he couldn't blame her for that. 'I'm a doctor. Is it all right if I take a look and access the damage?'

Her eyes locked with his. Forest-green eyes, reminding him of long-ago summers spent walking in the hills. 'The front edge of that boy's board slammed directly into my talus. The pain was instant and excruciating. It's broken.'

Talus, eh? Not ankle bone. Then she knew a medical thing or two. With a sinking stomach he studied the extended foot. She was also probably right about the fracture. Unless she'd twisted her ankle as she'd fallen. 'I apologise for this. My sons tend to be over-exuberant about everything they do.' Understatement of the year, but he wasn't about to spill his guts and tell this woman that most days he struggled to cope with their antics. That was none of her business even if they were to blame for her current predicament.

Wow, she's beautiful.

Where the hell had that come from? He glanced around, saw nothing out of the ordinary, no one speaking over his shoulder. He returned to looking at the woman, sucking in a groan of raw need. Despite the pain distorting her face, she was drop-dead stunning. *Do the job and get her packed up and on the way to hospital. Do not think about anything else. This might be one stunning female but the point is she is a female and therefore nothing but trouble.*

'They were in a hurry,' said the woman, easily distracting him. Then she shifted on her butt and gasped. Her knuckles whitened as she clenched her hands and waited for the pain to subside. Despite the situation her voice held a gentle lilt, in the way a Southlander spoke.

'Scottish ancestry?' Now, why had he asked that? None of his business, and nothing to do with this foot that needed to be eased out of a worn slip-on shoe.

'Not a drop. Growing up at the bottom end of the country tends to mean we don't speak like the rest of you kiwis.'

The roll of her 'r's tickled him, warmed him. He'd always been a sucker for women with accents. Yeah, and look where that had got him.

He instantly refocused on the rapidly swelling ankle. He shouldn't need any reminders about beautiful women with sexy accents and how shallow they could turn out to be. 'I'll call the ambulance crew. They'll have nitrous oxide on board for you to suck on while they remove your shoe.' The knowing glint in her eyes told him she knew what nitrous oxide was. 'Andrew, get my phone. Now.'

'Yes, Dad.'

'Marcus, bring the cushions from the couch out here for the lady.'

'Yes, Dad. But we—'

'Do as I say.' His calm tone belied his anxiety for this woman and the annoyance that just for once his boys could've held back on arguing with him.

'Very obedient,' muttered the woman, as the boys disappeared inside the house.

You think? 'Only because they know they're in deep trouble right at this moment.' Cam gently straightened her leg, making sure he didn't jar that ankle. 'I'm Cameron Roberts, by the way. A GP at the local medical centre. Make that the only GP at the centre.'

'Jenny Bostock.' Her full lips pressed flat, and the green of her eyes dimmed as she stared over his shoulder as though trying to focus on something other than her ankle. Her hair might've originally been tied back in that band now hanging down her back, but it must've sprung free when she'd gone tumbling down in a heap. Thick, red waves cascaded over her shoulders, down her back, even over one side of her face.

Resisting the urge to lift the hair back from her cheek wasn't as easy as it should've been. But following up on that impulse could get him struck off the medical practitioners' register, if not a slap across his face. 'Are you visiting Havelock for the day or stopping on the way through?' *I am not being nosy, merely trying to distract you while I tend to this painful ankle.*

Blinking, she refocused on him. 'I crossed over on the ferry this morning and decided to take Queen Charlotte Drive instead of going direct to Blenheim. Then at Havelock I decided to take a walk along the main street before having lunch at that café beside the marina.'

'My sons have put paid to that idea. I'm very sorry. They get a bit carried away at times.' The only place she was going now was hospital.

'Double trouble, eh?' Those lips lifted into the semblance of a smile, surprising and warming him. The anger had abated. Hardly surprising given what she was coping with. She'd be focusing on dealing with the pain.

'Forget that saying. Whoever made it up hadn't had twins of their own. Try tenfold trouble.' He grimaced, then dug deep for a smile of his own, the movement of his mouth a little strained. 'But on the plus side I get ten times the love.'

'They came skating out of nowhere. Don't be too hard on them. For all I know, this could've been my fault. I was watching a boat heading out of the marina and not looking where I was going.'

'You're being kind. I've told them more times than I can count to be very careful of pedestrians. Not that we get many this end of town.'

'They're boys—of course they're not going to listen to you.'

'Don't I know it.' Time to lock those skateboards away till they learned to control their actions. 'Any numbness?' Cam asked, as he lightly tapped her foot. When she nodded he continued with, 'Want to try and move your foot?'

'Not really.' But her lips flattened and her eyes took on a determined look.

He knew the moment she tried by the spike of pain in her eyes. 'Stop. I'm sure you're right about this not being a sprain.'

'Here's the phone.' Andrew appeared on the other side of Jenny.

'I got the cushions.' His other boy scuttled

along to join them, his arms laden with every cushion to be found in the house. Not many.

'Place them behind the lady one at a time. Careful. Don't bump her. You'll hurt her some more.' He wanted to growl at the boys, shout at them for being careless, but it seemed he did too much of that these days. His goal at the moment was to refrain from being a grump all the time. Maybe they'd learn from this accident without him reading them the riot act or banning the boards. They got so much fun out of skateboarding he hated to take that from them.

Jenny directed the placing of the cushions, talking softly to the boys like this happened to her every day. They lapped it up, tossing him a look that suggested he should be taking heed and learning something from this.

Standing up, Cam direct-dialled the volunteer ambulance chief. 'Hey, Braden, you're needed outside my gate. Lady with a suspected broken ankle needs pain relief and transport to Wairau.'

'Wairau?' Thick eyebrows rose as those forest eyes focused on him from down on the pavement.

His knees clicked as he hunched down again.

'Hospital in Blenheim. You need an X-ray and an orthopaedic surgeon's take on what that shows up.'

'There goes my catwalk career.' Was that a twinkle through the pain in her eyes?

Catwalk? Yep, come to think of it, those long, slim legs filling his view were made for modelling. *Thinking's not always wise*, said his brain, while his eyes cruised the length of her. The rest of her body was A1 too, topped off with that glorious hair and a face that could tempt a eunuch. *Which you pretty much are these days, boyo.* Given the chance, Jenny Bostock could certainly change his mind on avoiding the female half of the population. *So don't give her a chance.* He straightened up again, putting space between them. Hell, he was up and down like a yoyo.

Time to get practical. 'I presume you've got a car parked up somewhere around here. It can go in my garage until you're ready to drive again.' It was the least he could do, considering who'd had put her out of action.

Her fingers slid into the hip pocket of snug-fitting, mid-thigh-length shorts and tugged a key ring free. 'Red sports car, registration HGH 345, parked outside the woodcarver's.'

He nearly missed the keys as his gaze remained fixed on that hip. Catching them at the last moment, her words finally registered. Sports car, yeah, right. 'You're very trusting.' Which probably meant the vehicle was an old bomb in need of lots of repairs.

'Dr Cameron Roberts, Havelock GP. Shouldn't be too hard to track down. Anyway, I'm lying outside his front gate: 5C Rose Street.'

Far too observant. Just then he heard a siren. 'They're turning it on for you.'

'All ambos like to play with their bells and whistles, don't they? But I admit I'll be glad of that nitrous oxide. This is doing my head in.' A grimace tightened her mouth. She'd run out of smiles. Those bewitching eyes looked plain old tired now. Her attention to him and the boys had all been for show, something to take her mind off what was really happening.

'Should've asked you this sooner. Is there someone I can call for you? Get them to meet you at the hospital?'

Those eyes went blank as she withdrew completely. 'No, thanks.'

'You'll need to be picked up after the medical team has put you back together.'

'I'll sort it.' She looked away, but not before he saw desolation glittering out at the world. Then, 'Hi, guys. You come to get me? I hope you've brought lots of painkillers.'

Braden and his sidekick, Lyn, jogged over with a stretcher, a cardboard splint, their medical kit and the tank of gas Jenny was longing for.

Cam said, 'Hi, guys. Meet Jenny Bostock.' Guilt assailed him again, this time brought on by that desolation she was busy trying to hide, and knowing if it hadn't been for his sons she wouldn't be in whatever predicament she now found herself.

'Dad, can we go to the shops?'

'We saw Mum get out of a car at the end of the road.'

His heart crashed. They'd seen their mother? There was more likelihood of pigs flying by. Would this ever stop? As if it wasn't enough that they'd broken this woman's ankle, they thought they'd seen their selfish mother. When would the boys accept that that particular woman had no intention of ever returning? Even if she deigned to drop by because she'd had a rush of oxygen to the brain, she certainly would not want two eight-year-olds interfering with her career plans.

'There isn't time. You're meant to be at the softball juniors' Christmas party in an hour and you still have to clean your faces and put on decent clothes.'

The disappointment blinking out at him from two almost identical faces hurt as much as that broken ankle was hurting Jenny. Better he give it to them straight than have them walking up and down the short main street peering into every shop and café, looking for someone who was hundreds of k's away in the North Island. He hated having to be the big bad ogre breaking their hearts by telling them that when it was their mother who'd caused their anguish.

He looked away, his gaze encountering Jenny's as she drew in deep breaths of gas. This time he couldn't read the expression in those green eyes at all. He didn't try to guess because he wouldn't be seeing her again. Whatever she was thinking didn't matter.

Braden said, 'We'll be off as soon as we've got a splint on this here leg and loaded Jenny in the ambulance. You going to happy hour at the pub tonight?'

The fundraiser for the school swimming pool maintenance. 'That depends on what time the boys' Christmas do finishes and we get back here.' He and the kids had become experts at socialising, being invited to just about every celebration happening in Havelock. Anything from a cat's birthday to the theatre group's finishing night was an excuse to have fun around here. Which was fine, except when someone took it into their head to arrange a function in Blenheim, a thirty-minute drive away. Not far except when appointments were stacking up or, like at this time of year, there were too many social engagements to attend.

'Might see you later.' Braden and Lyn shifted their patient onto the stretcher and rolled her across to the ambulance.

Cam followed, unable to walk away. 'I hope all goes well for you at Wairau, Jenny. And once again, I'm sorry for my boys' actions.'

Removing the gas inhaler from her mouth, she

gave a semblance of a smile. 'Accidents happen all the time. I should've been looking where I was going.'

This woman was very quick to forgive. Not many people would've said that. A genuine, good-hearted lady? Or was the laughing gas mellowing that despair that had been glittering out from those suck-him-in eyes?

Watching the ambulance pull away and head towards the intersection, he felt a tug of longing he hadn't felt in years. Longing for what? Something about Jenny's bravery had caused it, made him feel he should be following in his car, going to the ED with her. Holding her hand? Yeah, right. Holding a beautiful woman's hand was so not on his agenda. He shrugged. Couldn't deny feeling responsible for her.

If there'd been someone with her, or even meeting her at the other end, he wouldn't be thinking like this. But it sounded like she was alone. So when she came out of hospital, where would she go? How would she get there? She hadn't been carrying a bag, wasn't wearing a jacket with pockets to hold money or credit cards. Or a phone. Just the keys she'd handed him to the car he had to retrieve and park at home. He swore, once, softly. He was going to have to deliver her bag to her.

He spied the boys carrying the cushions up the drive, flicking him worried looks from under their too-long hair, having obviously heard his bad language but not willing to tell him off as they normally did. At least they'd got the seriousness of the situation. He sighed. Time to get moving if they weren't to be late for the party.

Oh, and note to self: arrange for two haircuts at the hair salon on Monday afternoon after school.

CHAPTER TWO

JENNY STARED AROUND the ED and shivered. 'I want out of here. Like now.'

Not going to happen. The ED specialist had told her what she'd already suspected—that he was waiting for an orthopaedic surgeon to come in and look at her X-rays, and who knew when that would be. Apparently the surgeon had been out fishing on Queen Charlotte Sound when the ED staff had eventually got hold of him.

Waiting patiently wasn't her forte any more. And waiting in an ED was cruel. There'd been a time she'd loved nothing more than turning up for her shift in the emergency department. She'd thrived on the heightened anticipation brought on when waiting for the unknown to come through the doors, and by helping put people back together after some disaster had befallen them. 'Yeah, well, you turned out to be useless at that, didn't you?'

The ED was full to overflowing. The adjacent cubicle wasn't completely curtained off, leaving her open to scrutiny from a blue-eyed toddler with curls to die for. A young man lay on the bed in obvious pain, after apparently coming off his farm bike and being pinned underneath for an hour until his wife had found him. The injuries couldn't be life-threatening or he'd be in Theatre already.

'Up.' A very imperious tone for someone so young.

'No, Emma, leave the lady alone.' The child's mother snatched her out of reach to plonk her on a chair by the man's bed. 'I'm sorry about that,' said the harried woman.

'No problem.' Jenny dredged up a smile and watched as the little girl clambered off the chair the moment her mother's attention left her.

'You all right there?' asked a chirpy trainee nurse from the other side of Jenny's bed. Too happy for her own good. 'Anything I can get you?'

Didn't they teach nursing students not to tease their patients? 'I'd kill for a strong coffee right about now.'

'Nil by mouth, I'm sorry. At least until after Mr McNamara has seen you, and then only if you're not having surgery.'

'I totally get it. It's called wishful thinking.' Talk about getting more than her share of apologies today. Cameron Roberts had looked and sounded more than apologetic, with tiredness and stress blinking out at her from those coffee-brown eyes peeking from under a mass of wayward blond curls. Bet those gorgeous twins were more than a handful. Trouble and twins were synonymous. She had first-hand experience of that.

The nurse smoothed the already smooth bed-cover. 'If you want anything, call me. There are some magazines lying around somewhere but they're years out of date.'

'I'm fine.' She could pretend, couldn't she?

'Great.' The student flashed another smile and went to charm another patient, leaving her in relative peace to contemplate her situation. Which was looking rather dire.

Stuck. That's what she was. Stopped in her tracks, all because of a boy on an out-of-control skateboard. He'd wrecked everything. Like she'd slammed into a brick wall and there was no way round. She'd wanted to yell at those boys, tell them they should've been looking where they were going, not shouting and taunting each other to go faster. She did remember turning to see what the noise was about seconds before the boy—Marcus?—had crashed into her. But in all reality she'd been miles away, unaware of much except that boat heading out and the sun on her face.

The boys had looked so repentant. They'd also appeared as if they'd had enough of being told off and wanted to be given a break. She totally knew what that was like. How many times had she and Alison driven Mum insane with their mischief? Cameron Roberts hadn't known she knew what she was talking about. 'Bet I could teach those boys a thing or two about being naughty.'

Then an image of Cam's tired and frustrated expression slipped into her mind and she re-tracted that thought. The man didn't need any more problems.

'Emma? What's the matter, baby?' In the next cubicle the mother's panic was immediately apparent. 'Why's she gone so red? Emma. She's not breathing.'

Jenny swung her legs over the side of the bed, ground her teeth on the flare of pain. 'I'm a doctor. Pass her here.' One look at the child's terrified face, which only minutes ago had been grinning at her, had Jenny reaching back to slam her hand against the emergency button on the wall behind her bed. 'What was she playing with?'

'I'm not sure. Cotton balls, I think.'

Grabbing the child from the distraught mother's arms, Jenny ran a finger around the inside of her mouth, scooped out sodden cotton balls. Had the child swallowed any? 'Does Emma have any allergies that you know of?' she demanded.

'No.'

Emma definitely wasn't breathing. Instantly laying the child over her knees with her head hanging down, Jenny began striking the child firmly between the shoulder blades with the flat of her hand. Strike one. Two. Come on, baby. Breathe for me. Three. Please. Four. Please, please, please. Five. Where are the doctors?

Check the resp rate. The tiny chest wasn't moving at all.

Jenny knew the mother was screaming at her but she ignored her, focused on saving this little girl. Quickly standing on her good foot, ignoring the pain slicing up her leg, she held Emma around her waist and located her belly button with her finger.

'What's going on?' A doctor raced into the cubicle, followed by two nurses.

At last. But handing over now meant wasting precious seconds. Jenny fisted one hand. 'This child appears to have choked. No resp rate. I've done five back strikes.' Oh. Tell him. 'I am an ED doctor.' I *was* an ED doctor. Her fist thrust upward into Emma's abdomen. One. Two. Emma coughed hard and a small round object shot across the floor.

'A lid off a pill bottle by the look of it.' One of the nurses retrieved it from under the next bed.

The doctor took the now crying and bewildered child from Jenny's arms and laid her on the bed. 'Shh, sweetheart. You're going to be all right.' He looked over his shoulder at the crying woman and the frantic father trying to get off his bed. 'Mum? Come and hold your little girl while I examine her. What's her name?'

'Emma.' The mother scooped up her baby and held her tight.

'Easy. I need to give her a complete exam. Nurse, bring me a child's blanket. Jason, get back on that bed. You shouldn't be moving. You'll start that wound bleeding again.' The doctor turned back to his little patient and gave her a quick but thorough going over. 'She's going to be fine, thanks to this doctor.'

The mother had lost all colour in her cheeks. 'Thank you so much, all of you. If you hadn't done what you did…' She swallowed.

Jenny eased her butt back onto her bed. The pain in her ankle had intensified now that she wasn't being distracted. 'Don't go there,' she advised with a smile she hoped wasn't a grimace as pain stabbed repeatedly. 'Instead be glad you were here and not at home when it happened.'

Within minutes the department had returned to normal. Except for the hiccups in the next cubicle as the mother slowly calmed down, only muted voices could be heard once more.

With a sigh Jenny lay back. Talk about having the day from hell. But a broken ankle was low on the scale of urgency and really she was incredibly lucky. Euphoria nudged her despair aside. That child would've been saved by any of the doctors or nurses on duty but she'd done it. Her old instincts had kicked in instantly. She hadn't had to spend precious moments trying to recall the procedure. It had been there, lying in some unused corner of her brain waiting to be summoned.

It was good to know she still had it, even though she wasn't about to do anything stupid like go back to being a doctor. Yet the words 'I'm a doctor' had spilled off her tongue without thought. If she had stopped to consider that, she'd probably have handed Emma to another medic and lost precious seconds.

Wriggling further back against the pillows, she wondered what she'd do once she was discharged. Originally she'd planned on staying in Blenheim for a couple of nights and visiting the vineyards she'd gone to with Alison two years ago and having a glass of her sister's favourite bubbly.

Did she still stop here until she was capable

of getting around again? Doing what? Reading, eating, sleeping. Boring. What about going to Havelock? Her chuckle was humourless. Less than five hundred people lived there. So not her, a place like that. All too soon the locals would start saying hello, and then asking how her day was going. She shuddered. Face it. Stopping for more than three nights anywhere was so not her at the moment. But as of now she was no longer on the move.

Almost six months on the road hadn't solved anything, hadn't given her the forgiveness she ached for, hadn't brought her any closer to accepting what had happened.

This road trip had just about run its course anyway. There were only two more stops to go. Yeah, well, like climbing mountainsides in the Kahurangi National Park was going to happen now. Saying goodbye to Alison might have to wait another year.

Tears welled up, spilled down her face. 'So sorry, sis. I intended being at the place where you left me on the first anniversary.' Now that final goodbye had been taken from her in a sin-

gle hit. A little like Alison's death. One fall off
a mountainside and she'd gone. For ever.

'You look like you could do with some company.'

Now, that wasn't a memory. That voice was
from three hours ago. Ducking her head further down to hide her face, she croaked around
her clogged throat, 'Dr Cameron Roberts.' Who
didn't sound overly pleased to be here. Surprise,
surprise.

'You remembered, then. Most people call me
Cam.'

She'd always had a phenomenal memory. Right
down to the very last word Alison had ever said
to her. She drew a deep breath, and put Alison
to one side—for now at least. 'You can't find the
location of the boys' Christmas party?'

He sat on the edge of her bed without asking.
At least he was careful not to disturb her broken foot. 'Safely delivered and for once I'm not
putting on the red suit and handing out parcels
to over-excited kids.'

'Sounds like fun all round.' She looked up,
momentarily forgetting about her tears.

'Hey, you're crying.' He looked nonplussed, like crying women threw him.

Sure am. 'Guess it's just a reaction to finding myself in here, instead of enjoying that lunch down on the marina.' Telling a virtual stranger the truth would sound like she was looking for sympathy and that was the very last thing she intended. She didn't deserve it, for starters. 'Don't mind me. I'm fine, really.'

He looked relieved. Because the tears hadn't become a torrent? 'I hear you're waiting for Angus McNamara to show up.'

'Is he any good?' Like, hello? What choice did she have?

'You don't except me to say otherwise, do you?' Cam was still watching her closely, but now a small smile slowly appeared, like he wasn't used to smiling.

'Not really.' He should try the smile thing more often as it turned an already good-looking face into something beyond handsome. Her stomach sucked in and her heart knocked gently against her ribs, as if to say, Hey, sit up and take note. He's one cool dude. *Except, dear heart, the man has a wife. Those boys mentioned seeing their mother*. She shifted a little and groaned, grinding out, 'You'd tell me if I'd be better off seeing a chainsaw specialist, wouldn't you?'

Cam grimaced with her then told her, 'Angus is very good.' He swung her car keys between them. 'The car's parked in my garage, out of the way. I brought in your case. Thought you'd want a change of clothes some time.' Thoughtful as well as a hunk. 'It's in the ED office until they know whether you're having surgery or just getting a proper splint and crutches.'

'Would you mind putting the keys in my case? Losing them would only give me another headache to deal with.'

'Sure.' Cam stared thoughtfully at a spot somewhere around his feet. 'If you're discharged, where will you go?'

She had no idea. 'Yesterday I looked up motels in Blenheim and found heaps of vacancies so I didn't bother making a booking. I'll phone around when I know what's going on here.'

'You sure that's what you want to do? You could catch a flight home as soon as they kick you out of here.' The question in his eyes asked where home was.

She wasn't answering it. 'I'll be fine. Lots of options, really.' She played mental ping-pong. A motel where she'd have to get take-out delivered because of her inability to move around? Or a flight out to where? Which town would she settle in and pretend it felt like home until she was okay to move on again? According to some, home was where the heart was, and her heart was lost right now.

At the moment all her worldly possessions were locked up in a container in a storage yard in Auckland, no doubt going mouldy. She suspected that after her road trip she'd like somewhere new to start again.

'I'll leave you my numbers so you can call me if you want anything else out of your car.'

'Thanks.' The carton of medical journals could wait a month or so. The hiking boots, running shoes and camping gear were absolutely useless at the moment. Blink, blink. *Stop feeling sorry for yourself. It's a broken ankle, not a catastrophe, even if you are stuck here for a while.* Her gaze drifted to Cam, over his expansive chest and on down to the long legs stretched half across the cubicle. 'How did you manage to get behind the steering wheel of my car? Your knees must've been up around your ears.'

'That's something I'm used to. Though driving a sports car was a novelty, even if only for half a kilometre. The boys couldn't believe what they were seeing when I pulled up at home.'

'I can picture their faces.' She continued checking him out. *Why?* She had no idea.

This guy spent time in the sun. His skin had a mouth-watering tan. Those calf muscles were well honed. Her stomach squeezed. *Settle.* The last thing she needed right now was to get interested in a man. She had nothing to offer anyone. She ran on empty all the time. Anyway, this particular man was taken. *Remember?* Remember. 'You look fit. You run?' Why was she even asking? He'd disappear any minute and that would be the end of that.

Surprise widened his eyes. 'It's the one thing that keeps me sane some days.'

She'd focus on his running, nothing else. 'That can't be easy with only a handful of short streets or the main highway to pound out on.' An hour in Havelock had been ample time to get the idea of how small the place was.

'I use Queen Charlotte Drive. The hill's a bit of a grunter but the traffic moves at a far slower pace than out on the main road. Sometimes the boys cycle with me. I'd never take them on the main road. Too many large trucks rolling through all the time.'

'Your boys are cute.' Where was their mother? Had she gone to the party with them?

'Don't you dare tell them that. They absolutely hate anyone using the "cute" word.' Another smile, more expansive this time, lifted his mouth into a delicious curve and lightened the brown of his eyes.

'They're strong-willed?'

Cam nodded his head slowly. 'Unfortunately, yes.'

'You'd want your kids to be pushovers?' she asked, wondering exactly why he'd dropped by. She wasn't his patient or his friend.

His sigh filled with sadness as the smile switched off and his gaze dulled. 'They're a funny mix of strong and soft. Kind of nice, I guess, but there are things I wish they were stronger about.'

If only she knew how to wipe away that look,

bring back the warm smile. But it wasn't her place. They were strangers who were going to remain so. 'I'm sure all parents think that.' How enlightening. Not.

'You got kids?' His question was nothing startling, fitted into their conversation, and yet it arrowed in for her heart.

'No.' She'd always hoped she'd get married and have a family. That had been part of her life plan, along with the medical career, the extended travel to Europe and watching Alison achieve her goal to become an international airline pilot. Except Alison had died because *she* had failed as a doctor. Her new life plan was waiting to be rewritten, but one thing she knew for certain was that having a family would be a part of it. Losing her sister had heightened that need.

'Hello, Cam. Didn't expect to find you here. You know my patient?' A middle-aged man strode around the curtain and stopped at the end of her bed.

'Not really. My boys are responsible for this. A skateboarding accident of no mean proportions.'

'Ouch.' The casually presented man turned to her. 'I'm Angus, your surgeon.'

She held out her hand. 'Jenny Bostock. Should I be asking if you caught any fish? Or will that make you go a little harder on me?' Plastering on a smile she didn't feel much like making, she watched closely to see how he reacted to her.

'Your timing was perfect. Dinner's ready and waiting in the fridge at home. Blue cod. The best fish in our waters, as far as I'm concerned.' His friendly smile faded. 'I've seen your X-rays. The lower tibia has a fine fracture, but it's the talus that needs attending to, I'm afraid. You require plates to be attached.'

'That's what I expected.' And didn't want. But there was nothing she could do about it, except rewind the clock four hours and stay in her car, instead of walking around Havelock.

'Do you want me to outline the whole procedure, *Dr* Bostock?' The surgeon emphasised her title.

Beside him, Cam lifted his eyebrows. 'So you are a doctor. I wondered if you were.'

'Angus has been reading my admission slip.' She should've put dog walker or cleaning lady but some habits didn't disappear, even after six months. 'Anyway, it was irrelevant to the situation. I'm presuming you'd have treated me the same, no matter what my job was.'

Cam shrugged. 'Of course.'

She didn't go around telling anyone she was a doctor. People might ask her to treat them or give them advice, and they really didn't need that from her. But when it came to filling in paperwork she tended to honest. Just in case she ever got her life back on track.

'Jenny—I can call you that?' The surgeon's eyebrow rose in query.

'Sure.'

'Jenny's being coy. I'm surprised you haven't heard how she saved a child who was choking not more than thirty minutes ago. Everyone's talking about her.'

Cam's eyes widened. 'Truly? That's awesome. I have to say you seem to have a habit of finding yourself in the middle of trouble. Is that usual? Or is today the exception?'

Define trouble. Crossing her fingers, she muttered, 'It's been one of those days when I shouldn't have got out of bed.'

'Well, you're back in one now.' Cam's smile

was cheeky, warming her where she didn't want to be warmed. Right around her heart.

'Right.' Angus became brisk. 'Let's get this under way. The anaesthetist should be here any minute. I'll head over to Theatre and wait for you there.' He flicked the curtain wide to stride out.

Cam took his cue. 'I'd better go and check on those boys of mine, see what other mischief they've managed to get themselves into.'

She called after him, 'Thanks for dropping by. I'll sort out what to do about my car when I'm a bit more mobile. I'll give you a buzz some time tomorrow. Is that okay?'

'It can stay where it is for weeks, if necessary. Call me if you want anything else.' He was only being helpful to a stranger for whom his boys had caused trouble. It was there in his eyes, in the now flat smile he gave.

'Thanks.' Suddenly she didn't want him to go. Her fingers picked at the sheet covering her. The idea of being anaesthetised made her feel tetchy. All the what-if scenarios popped into her mind. Surgery was not without its risks. *So talk to Cam, ask him questions about anything at all to keep him here for a bit.*

'I can hang around until Sheree gets here.' So he read minds.

'Sheree?'

'The anaesthetist on duty this weekend.' His butt sank back onto the edge of the bed. 'In what field of medicine do you practise?'

The down side of having him stay was fielding the unwanted questions. 'Emergency.'

'You feel weird, being an ED patient?' Those eyebrows rose again.

Kind of cute when they did that. Did *he* like the 'cute' word? Why was she even asking herself that? The man had a family, wasn't available. But it had been a long time since she'd been interested in a man that way. 'Not weird, just scary being on the receiving end of all the attention.'

'I had keyhole surgery for appendicitis ten months ago. If it hadn't been for the pain and knowing how fast the whole thing could've turned bad, I'd have bailed out of having the operation. Call me a wimp, but I knew everything that was going to happen, and that made it worse.'

'You mean you understood what could go wrong.' Like she did.

A big, warm hand covered hers. 'You'll be fine. Sheree and Angus know what they're doing. The worst of this will come afterwards, when you can't get around easily. I could send my boys in to be your slaves for as long as it takes to get back on your feet.' His brow crinkled. 'They're not very good at cooking, or cleaning, or making decent coffee. Great at fetching and carrying, though.'

Surprised he could joke with her, the nervousness took a step back. 'You make them sound like puppies. Fetch, Booboo.' The warmth seeping into her from that small contact made her relax even more. Then she tensed. Tugged her hand free. *He has a wife.* 'Thanks for your concern, but I'm fine. Really.'

Cam's gaze cruised over her face, studying her intently. Looking for what? Then with a brief nod he stood up. 'I can hear Sheree talking out there. I'll head away. Take care.'

She stared at the curtain long after he'd gone. What would it be like to have Cameron Roberts to come home to at the end of a busy day in the department? *Excuse me, you don't work in an ED any more. You don't work at all. As for coming home to that particular man, you must be high on laughing gas. He's taken, remember?*

A girl was allowed to dream, wasn't she?

CHAPTER THREE

JENNY WOKE TO a nurse pumping a blood-pressure cuff wrapped around her arm. 'Did I miss the party?'

The nurse frowned. 'Party?'

'The dry mouth and fuzzy head.'

An easy smile. 'The revolting after-effects of anaesthetic. Your blood pressure's normal. I need to take your temperature.' A thermometer was slipped into her mouth as the nurse continued to talk. 'Breakfast will be along shortly. You've got visitors, too.'

'Visitors?' Jenny spluttered around the glass stick between her lips. 'I don't know—' Anyone except Cam and his boys. 'Oh.'

'Those boys are so gorgeous.' Then the girl winked. 'Just like their dad.'

'True.' It had to be post-op trauma that made her agree. 'Does Mr McNamara do rounds on Sundays?'

'He phoned earlier to say he'd drop by to see you this morning.'

'Hey, sunshine, you're looking more comfortable,' Cam called from the doorway. 'Up to visitors? As in three of us?'

'You bet.' Shuffling up the bed, she pulled the sheet up to her throat and settled back on the pillows the nurse rearranged at her back. Sunshine, eh? More like a disaster zone, with hair that hadn't been brushed and probably yesterday's mascara making dark smudges under her eyes. But it felt inordinately good to see him.

Cam stepped into the tiny room, followed by his sons carefully carrying coffee and something smelling suspiciously like a hot croissant.

'Hello, guys. Is that for me?'

They nodded in unison. 'Yes.'

'You're crackerjacks, you know that? I've been hanging out for a proper coffee since I arrived in this place.' To think she could've blown this by venting her anger at them yesterday.

'There's a bacon and egg thing, too.' One of them held out the bag to her.

'Bacon and egg croissant,' the other explained.

'Okay, tell me, is there a trick to knowing

who's Marcus and who's Andrew?' They were darned near identical, though now that she was looking for differences she could see one of the boys had a tiny scar on his chin. Tapping it gently, she asked, 'What happened there?'

'Marcus pushed me off the swing when we were little.'

'Gotcha. You're Andrew.' Now all she had to do was remember to look for that pale scar every time she bumped into these two scallywags. Like how often would that happen?

Andrew smiled a bigger, more impish version of that smile his father had given her yesterday when he'd visited the ED. 'Marcus has got a scar on his bottom.'

'Have not.' The other twin stuck his chin out and glared at his brother.

'Have too.' Andrew scowled and made to haul his brother's shorts down.

Cam stepped in. 'That's enough, boys. We came to visit, not turn the ward into a war zone.'

Jenny felt something oddly like laughter beginning to bubble up. When was the last time she'd laughed? 'Better than the boring place it

is at the moment. So how was your party? Did Santa Claus bring presents?'

'Santa Claus isn't real. He's—'

'Just an old man dressed up funny.'

Her breath hitched. A lump blocked her throat. She and Alison used to finish each other's sentences. Oh, boy, this just got hard. Harder. *Think of something to say. They're all staring at you.* 'Bet you accepted the presents he gave you.'

'Of course. They are cool. I got a remote-control plane.'

'I got a helicopter.'

'Pilots, eh? Have you been flying in real planes?' She wanted to tell them how cute they were but knew not to if she wanted to remain friends with them, and, strangely, despite that little glitch over the way they shared sentences, she found she did. Though the chances of seeing them again once they walked out of here were very remote.

Cam was shaking his head at the three of them. 'Don't any of you come up for air?'

All three of them shook their heads and smiled at Cam, who said, 'Great, so I'm the only sensible, sane one around here. Jenny, do you want milk for your coffee? Sugar? I can scrounge some off the nurses.'

'Milk and sugar would be good.'

'Dad, can we bring our presents to show her?' Marcus—or was it Andrew?—asked. They weren't directly facing her so there were no identifying marks in sight.

'The lady has a name. Miss...' His brow wrinkled as he glanced at her hands. 'Miss Bostock, or Dr Bostock.'

Jenny locked gazes with him, and felt a nudge in the pit of her stomach. He really was gorgeous. She hadn't been imagining it through the haze of nitrous oxide. 'I'm happy with Jenny, unless you object.' Definitely not Dr. She didn't deserve that title any more.

He shrugged. 'No problem. Okay, lads, give Jenny the food and coffee. No, don't climb on the bed. She has a very sore foot.'

Instantly Marcus's smile disappeared and his head dropped forward. 'I'm sorry.'

So was she, but it had happened and grumping about it wouldn't make him feel good. Wouldn't do her any favours either. Leaning forward, she raised the boy's head with her hand under his chin so he had to look at her. 'Listen to me. It was an accident. You didn't mean it, did you?' His head slid from side to side. 'You didn't see me and I didn't see you. I was watching the fishing boat out on the water. So let's not worry about this again. Okay?'

Marcus nodded and looked at his dad. 'She's nice, Dad. I like her.'

Heat seeped into her cheeks, probably making her usually pale face resemble a stop light. That was the nicest thing anyone had said to her in a long while. She could even feel tears collecting in the back of her eyes. Great. Crying twice in less than twenty-four hours. Cam would think she should be in the mental health ward and rush his boys away.

'Breakfast time,' called an older woman, as she pushed in a cart that rattled with plates and cups.

Saved by the cart. 'Can I have some milk and sugar, please?'

'Certainly. Your family brought in some decent coffee for you. That's lovely. Here, lads, hand Mum the milk, will you?'

Marcus stared at the woman with his mouth open and something like anguish in his brown eyes, while Andrew took the plastic bottle and passed it to Jenny, looking bemused but not upset.

'She's not our mother,' he informed the woman. 'She hurt herself on our skateboard so we're visiting.'

'That's nice of you. Is that breakfast in that bag? It will probably be tastier than the cereal I've got here for Dr Bostock.' With the number of patients she saw every day the woman would be used to making similar mistakes.

Cam finally got a word in. 'Jenny, do you want the hospital breakfast? We won't be insulted if you do.'

She shook her head. 'Just the milk and sugar, thanks, Sadie.' A quick read of the name badge pinned to the woman's ample chest earned her another smile.

'Here you go, then.'

Then another voice spoke from the doorway. 'Good morning, Jenny.' Angus strolled into the room, dressed in light slacks and a T-shirt. 'Morning, Cam, boys. How's everyone today?'

It was getting to be like a bus station in here. She looked around, found everyone watching her, waiting for her to answer. 'I'm good. Not that I've got out of bed yet so I've no idea how I'll go on crutches.'

'Crutches?' The twins' eyes lit up.

She grinned at them. Their innocent sense of fun made her feel good about a lot of things. 'It's going to be exciting driving my car, don't you think?'

'Time we left Jenny alone.' Cam headed for the door. 'She's got to talk to Mr McNamara.'

Disappointment tugged. With all the chatter between her and the twins Cam hadn't said a lot, and now she wished for a rerun of the minutes they'd all been here. This time she'd talk to Cam, find out more about living in Havelock, just because it would be a safe subject and she could listen to his deep, husky voice. But they were already on the way through the door, the boys pushing each other.

'Cam,' she called. 'Thanks for dropping by. I appreciate it.'

He turned a steady gaze her way, that anguish under control. 'I could leave the boys with you for the day if you want company.'

I'd like that. I really would. They're gorgeous

fun. One day, Jenny, one day in the distant future. 'Guess the ward staff might have something say about that.'

'So would you after the first hour. We'd better not keep Angus waiting. He's dressed for golf, I'd say.'

'You're not wrong, Cam. I won't be long with Jenny if you want to wait.'

Cam shook his head. 'We've got things to do in town. I want to be done and home before the temperature really cranks up. It's hot out there already.' Cam turned to her again. 'See you later.'

Really? He'd drop by again? She nodded, afraid if she spoke the sudden lump in her throat might dissolve into tears. She was so used to being on her own it was like being knocked in the back of the knees to have had the Roberts trio turn up here to see her. Watching Cam walk away, she drank in the sight of his broad shoulders and a very tidy butt clad in khaki chinos.

Angus cleared his throat and she turned her attention back to him. 'What happens next? Am I out of here this morning?'

'Have you got anywhere to go?'

'Yes.' They had taxis in Blenheim, didn't they?

The surgeon was shaking his head. 'You'll have to do better than that. Your admittance form gave a post box number—in Dunedin.'

Caught. 'I'm staying in a motel.'

'Which one?'

Hell. What was the name of one she'd checked out on line two days ago? The Grape Castle? The Vineyard Retreat? Her shoulders slumped. 'I'll make a booking before I leave here.'

'That will be tomorrow at the earliest. If you had someone to take care of you I'd discharge you today, but I don't want you tottering around on your own until you've got the hang of using crutches. Anyway, you shouldn't be walking anywhere, even across a room, until the swelling's gone down, and I suspect checking into a motel would involve more movement than I would be happy with.'

'Give me all the gory details and then go and enjoy that round of golf. I'll stay put. For now.'

The look he gave her suggested he didn't trust her to behave. Neither did she, but she'd keep that to herself. By the time Angus had filled her in on the operation and written a prescription for painkillers she no longer had the energy to get out of bed. Round one to the surgeon.

The moment they got home Cam headed for the third, and rarely used, bedroom. He'd made his mind up. It was probably the dumbest thing he'd contemplated in a long line of dumb things but, hey, he'd do it anyway. 'Guys, come and give me a hand.'

Marcus and Andrew appeared in the doorway in a flash. 'What are you doing, Dad?'

'I want you to take all these books and toys and store them in your bedroom. In the back of the wardrobe if necessary.'

'Why?' came the usual question.

Because he'd seen despair in Jenny Bostock's eyes at the mention of sorting out what to do with her car tomorrow when she'd no doubt be feeling like hell on crutches. Plus because she seemed filled with sadness and loneliness, something he could understand. What he should be taking notice of was that restless expression that trawled through her gaze at times.

That expression he'd seen all too often in Margaret's eyes in the months before she'd packed

her bags and left them, except Margaret had
been more of a caged lioness waiting to attack
the world, whereas Jenny looked lost. A few
days bunked down in Havelock wouldn't hurt
her. His heart sighed. As long as that didn't hurt
him.

There was something indefinable about Jenny
that teased him. Beyond her physical attributes,
that was. Despite that frailty he sensed a self-
lessness and a need to put things right. Would a
woman like that walk out on her man after vow-
ing to love him for ever?

'Dad, why are we cleaning this room?'

'Because I'm going to ask Jenny if she'd like
to stay with us for a while.'

'Yay, that's cool.' The boys leapt into the air
and high-fived each other. 'We like her.'

'She didn't tell us off or get mad or anything
like that.'

That was the final reason he'd invite her. A
thank-you and an apology. 'You're very lucky
she's such an understanding lady.' He was curious why she hadn't immediately revealed to
him that she was a doctor. Had something gone
wrong with a case that had led to that sadness

leaking out of her eyes and dulling her face when she'd thought no one was watching her? It would have to be bad for her to stop practising, if that's what she'd done. It was a rocky road at times, being a doctor.

Cam picked up a pile of books and handed them to Marcus. 'Put those away.'

Andrew lifted an even bigger pile and staggered after his twin. Warmth stole through Cam. They really were great kids. If only he didn't get so tired and busy, and forget that sometimes.

Within minutes they were back scooping up armloads of toys and traipsing out again. Getting ahead of him and what he had to do to make this room habitable for Jenny. Even as he pulled off the bedcovers and began spreading freshly laundered sheets the doubts nudged at the corner of his mind. What if he was making an idiot of himself? Jenny might think he was making a move on her and that would lead to all sorts of difficulties. But, seriously, the most likely scenario would be her laughing and telling him she could manage on her own.

She probably could, but her vulnerability had nudged him, made him sit up and take notice,

had got him trying to read what was going on behind those beautiful big eyes she'd often turned
on him. Eyes that turned him on. Talk about another reason not to invite her here.

'Do I need this when I've already got more to
cope with than I can manage?' But guilt was a
heavy taskmaster. He owed her. 'You sure that's
what's behind this mad idea?'

'What did you say, Dad?'

'Talking to myself. Sorry, mate.' He might be
overloaded with work and kids, but he couldn't
walk away from Jenny. He'd invite her to come
to Havelock, and then it was up to her.

*Lighten up, Cameron. You are entitled to some
fun, too.* Really? *Really.*

Note to self: ask Mrs Warner to do the grocery shopping earlier this week in case there's
an extra mouth to feed.

'Where do you think you're going?' Cam shoved
his hands in his pockets and rested a shoulder
against the doorframe of Jenny's hospital room,
watching as she leaned against the bed. So slim,
yet physically as strong as a whippet. The frailty
was in her eyes, not her body.

Her head shot up so fast he heard vertebrae click, saw her wince. 'Don't sneak up on me like that.' Guilt darkened those green eyes glittering at him fiercely, reminding him of the sea when the kahawai were churning it up as they chased smaller fish.

'You were so engrossed in being stealthy you didn't hear me coming along the ward.' He couldn't hold back his smile any longer. It had been growing from the moment he'd seen her juggling her crutches and trying to pick up her bag from the chair. Which really should be a warning to hightail it out of there, instead of getting involved with her. He should be thinking apology here, not getting up close and interested in Jenny Bostock, pretty woman and sometime doctor.

'I was not.' Her turn to smile, though hers appeared very strained.

Shaking his head at her, he crossed to pick up her case himself. 'Give up arguing with me. I live with two experts, remember?'

'Where are you taking my case?' All pretence of smiling disappeared. 'Seriously, Cam, what do you think you're doing?'

'Taking you home.' So much for finesse. That must've gone down the plughole with the dish-water that morning. Had he thought he could railroad her into coming along quietly? If he had then he needed a brain scan. 'We have a spare bedroom available. You can hole up there for as long as you like. Once you're mobile again, as in using those crutches with more aptitude, we have cafés and a bakery, jewellery and fudge shops, all for you get lost in for hours on end.'

'I don't do shops. Not lately, at any rate. Though the café could be a plus.' Bewilderment etched her face. Maybe a bit of hope was in there, too. 'Is there a motel in Havelock?'

Had he really expected her to be thrilled about this? 'Backpackers' accommodation only.'

'Oh.' Her gaze dropped from him to her case and then to her crutches. She seemed to be weighing up her options.

He helped her along with making up her mind. 'The boys have got your room ready. They're really excited about having a visitor, even a prac-tically useless one who won't be playing cricket on the front lawn any time soon.'

'You play dirty.' Her forefinger tapped the handle of one of the crutches.

Not normally, but he couldn't walk out of here leaving Jenny to her own devices. She was ill prepared to go it alone for the next few days. 'Trying to make it easier for you to accept. You can leave any time you like, straight after dinner if you want to.'

'I see.' Tap, tap, tap went her finger on the crutch. 'What about your wife? Or did you bully her into this as well?'

Now who was playing dirty? 'I'm divorced.' Was he a slow learner, or what? Jenny was gorgeous, but she might not be any more trustworthy than his ex had been. So what? This was going to be a brief stay, not a lifelong one.

She sucked in air. 'I'm sorry, but I needed to know. Not about your divorce but that I wasn't treading on anyone's toes.'

'You're not treading on anything at the moment,' Cam quipped, in an effort to dispel his unease, but then thoughtlessly asked, 'You heard the boys saying they'd seen their mother yesterday?'

'Yes.'

'They hadn't. She lives in Auckland, last I heard.' That's all she needed to know. Probably out-of-date news anyway.

'That must be hard for all of you. Do they make a habit of seeing their mum in places she's not?'

'Unfortunately, yes. Margaret—my ex—left rather abruptly two years ago.' That's definitely all he was saying. Jenny had cleverly sidetracked him from his mission. 'Jenny, you are in a bind, partly due to my sons' antics. I don't know why you don't want to go home, wherever that is, but I'm more than happy to help you out until you're up and running again. That's all I'm offering. Though be warned, life in our house is hectic and noisy, but during the day you'll have peace and quiet while the boys are at school. Take it or leave it.'

He studied her small case. She travelled light, if this and what was in her car was anything to go by. His sisters would think Jenny needed lessons on what to take away on a trip, but then she'd need a truck, not a sports car.

She swung the crutches, took two wonky steps.

Her eyes locked with his as she tipped her head to one side. Sizing him up?

He went for broke, lifted the case and headed for the door. 'Coming?'

The silence was deafening. He kept walking, slowly so that if she decided to join him she wouldn't feel compelled to hurry. Why so little luggage? Those medical journals in her boot were hardly scintillating reading for a trip.

Clump, thump. She was moving, hopping on those sticks. Clump, thump.

Cam relaxed and kept walking, slowing even more.

Clump, thump.

Warmth spread through him. Jenny was coming home with him. He hadn't realised how much he wanted this until faced with the real possibility she'd turn him down. Being pushy had worked.

'I guess Havelock is as good a place to be as Blenheim.'

'Better, as far as I'm concerned. More community spirited.' Something he'd come to appreciate. It had taken time for him to get used to living in such a small place after spending ten years in Wellington. Nowadays he doubted he'd cope with the stress of city living with two young boys to keep a firm hand on.

'Only until I've got the hang of these damned things.' Bang, bang, the crutches slammed down on the floor. 'A couple of days at the most.'

'Sure.' The warmth spread. He'd asked out of guilt and yet now he was feeling good about the whole situation. *Steady, boy, steady. You might've leapt into the deepest part of the pond and have no way of surviving.*

'There she is.'

'Hello, Jenny. Are you coming to our house?' The twins mobbed her, threatening her precarious balance.

But before Cam got a word out Jenny was laughing with them and saying, 'How can I refuse that welcome?'

He hadn't got a laugh, or even a thank you. Did he need to take lessons from his sons on how to get onside with a pretty woman?

'Boys, wait here with Jenny while I bring the car to the door. Mind those crutches, will you?'

As he stepped out into the sunshine he heard

Marcus asking, 'Can we have a go on the crutches later? They're cool.'

Unfortunately the doors slid shut before he heard Jenny's reply, but something told him she'd have agreed. She got on with the boys so easily. As long as she didn't get too close and they got hurt when she left. He'd knew too well the devastation their mother had caused them when she'd walked away. But what were the odds Jenny would stay more than a night, two at the most? How attached could Marcus and Andrew get in that short time?

How attached would he get? He so wasn't ready to trust his heart again. Doubted he ever would be.

No getting away from the fact this had definitely been the dumbest idea he'd ever come up with. Not once had he factored the boys' hearts into the equation, let alone his own. *Blast you, Margaret, for doing this to us.* How long did it take for youngsters to truly understand what being abandoned by their mother meant? Or did they already get it and this searching for her was just part of the acceptance process?

Note to self: go see a shrink and get my head

space tidied up so I understand my boys and don't make stupid mistakes about a woman with beautiful eyes that I could drown in.

CHAPTER FOUR

'I've never been treated like royalty before.' Jenny smiled at the twins as a glass of chilled water slid onto the top of the small table beside the chair she'd been banished to. At least the lounge, dining area and kitchen all ran together so she didn't feel isolated from what everyone was up to. 'I could get used to this.'

'Dad said we had to make you—'

'Comfortable and get anything you need.'

Cam spoke from behind the kitchen counter. 'That also means not bothering Jenny all the time.'

Jenny spoke up before an argument ensued. 'Guys, maybe we could play a game on the computer or something later?'

The boys high-fived each other and shouted 'Yes' at the tops of their voices.

Cam nodded at them. 'That means you can go outside to play now.'

She watched them scrambling over each other in their haste to go out into the yard, then asked Cam, 'Do they ever slow down?'

'Exhausting to watch, aren't they?' That half smile appeared as his gaze followed his sons. 'You look sleepy. Do you want to go to bed for a while?'

That had to be the most uninviting invitation to bed she'd ever had. How would that deep, gravelly voice sound if he was really asking her to take a romp in bed? And why did she even want to know? Shaking her head abruptly, she looked up into the steadiest brown gaze she'd seen in a long time. A hint of amusement shone out at her. Had he picked up on her reaction to his question? Probably. Ouch.

'Jenny? You're space tripping.' His gaze was still locked with hers. Odd, really. Usually people who knew her and what had happened tended to look away. But, then, Cam hadn't a clue about her life up until yesterday.

'If it's all the same to you I'll stay right where I am. If I do nod off, don't insist on the boys being quiet. That'd make me feel bad.' She'd caused enough trouble for this family already.

'We're having a barbecue. Steak all right with you?'

'Perfect. Can I make the salad?' Though right at this moment telling the difference between a tomato and a cucumber might be difficult.

Her question got her a small smile. 'I don't think so.'

'Had to offer.' Actually, she felt glad he'd turned her down. Those crutches were turning out to be a little trickier to master than she'd have believed. His kitchen was safer without her clunking around in there.

'Is there anything you don't like to eat?' Cam asked.

'Tripe, Brussels sprouts and broad beans.'

'You're more than safe here.'

As Cam dug around in the pantry she studied his back view and found it still very delectable now her brain was clear of drugs and post-op fog. But, of course, finding herself here with a man she barely knew, she was bound to be over-reacting to all sorts of things. Then Cam turned to place bottles of sauces on the counter and caught her staring.

'Yes?' His eyebrows rose, and that smile hovered on his mouth.

Definitely ouch. Heat crept up her throat and spread across her cheeks. Caught, like a teenager ogling the teacher as he wrote on the board. 'Nothing.' Glancing around, she hurried to find something neutral to talk about. 'You've got a lovely home. Spacious and light, warm and cosy.' *Home and Garden* reporter she was not. 'Been here long?'

'Two and a half years. I was looking for a less hectic work schedule. On a holiday at the family farm out in the sounds, someone mentioned Havelock needed a GP. So here we are.'

'Is there enough work for a full-time doctor?' The town was less than small.

'I do mornings here four days a week and the rest of my time in Blenheim at the practice this one's linked to.'

'How do you manage? A GP's life is never quiet. Then there are your kids.'

'Solo parenting is a balancing act but I wouldn't

swap it for anything.' He sprinkled oil onto the steaks and reached for the pepper grinder.

As she watched those strong hands twisting the utensil, her stomach did a wee shake. Long, strong fingers. It didn't take any effort to imagine them tripping over her skin. Her cheeks burned like a furnace. In fact, her whole body had come alive.

'Did I knock my head when I fell yesterday?'

Instantly Cam was wiping his hands and coming towards her. 'Have you got a headache?' There was nothing but concern on his face, bringing her up short as he stared into her eyes. Looking for signs of concussion?

Abruptly shaking her head to break that searching look—who knew what he'd see in there?—she curled in on herself and muttered, 'Sorry. Not a headache.' Though one was beginning to tap behind her eyes. 'I didn't mean to say that out loud.'

That concern didn't lift. 'I think you're a dab hand at downplaying situations. So, do you have a headache or not?'

'No. Promise.' Just a dose of reawakened hormones. No problem. They'd soon get tired of not being let out to play and go back to their cave. But Cam wasn't moving away so some explanation was apparently expected. Like what? Where were the twins when she needed their boisterous exuberance? 'Promise,' she reiterated, and tried for nonchalance as she lifted the glass of water. For the life of her she couldn't think of anything to say that wouldn't have him packing her back into that four-wheel drive of his and delivering her to that backpackers' lodge up the road.

Finally he moved away, returned to his bench and dinner preparations. 'You didn't mention hitting your head yesterday, neither did you show any signs of a bang on the skull when I checked you out.'

'As I thought.' Sipping the refreshing water, she stared into the bottom of the glass. When was the last time she'd held a man, or been held in strong male arms? When was the last time she'd shared a kiss? Months ago, weeks before she and Colby had split.

Colby. A man driven by his background of poverty, he didn't know when to stop and enjoy what he'd achieved. He'd always wanted more, and had expected her to be into all that too.

When she'd mentioned that one day she hoped to have a family, he'd regarded her as if he didn't know her at all. Maybe he hadn't known who she'd become. Face it, she struggled to recognise herself sometimes. The one definite to come from losing Alison was that she wanted children. But first she had to find a man with the same beliefs and objectives. An image of a firm butt in fitting trousers flicked into her mind.

There hadn't been a man, any man, since Colby. Hadn't been the need. During her grand tour of places she and Alison had been it had left little energy or inclination for sex and romance. Anyway, sex with strangers so wasn't her thing, and she hadn't stopped anywhere long enough to get to know anyone. Until now. Again an image of Cam floated across her mind, this time a smiling, helpful Cam.

She jerked upright in the chair. Something cold and wet trickled over her stomach. The glass in her hand was empty. 'Did I nod off?'

'You did.' A large hand removed the glass. 'Want a replacement?' Cam asked, a hint of amusement in his voice.

Who could blame him? The guy already had

two kids to mind, he didn't need a delinquent adult as well. 'No, thanks.'

'Dad, we're hungry.'

'Now, there's surprise. Go and wash your hands, then set the table on the deck.'

'Is Jenny coming outside with us?'

Cam raised one eyebrow. 'I can bring your dinner in here if you like.'

'I don't think so.' She made to push up from the armchair and there was a steadying hand on her elbow. 'I'll join you out there.'

'Easy.' Cam handed her the blasted crutches.

'I could've hopped,' she growled, as she tucked the poles under her armpits and tried to balance without tipping over into a heap.

'You could have, and it would've hurt.' That was such a doctor tone.

She tried glaring at him. 'You have all the answers, don't you?' Then a smile broke over her mouth. It was impossible to be mad at him when he was being so kind and downright appealing.

'You'd better believe it.' Finally, those lips lifted into a return smile.

This time, thankfully, those hormones stayed in their cave. But warmth trickled through her.

When Cam smiled it was like a light in a black-out. Even though he didn't do full-blown, face-crinkling smiles, what he did give was rare and special, making her feel special. Which, of course, she wasn't. Not to Cam anyway.

She headed for the deck, carefully manoeu-vring around furniture. No way was she tipping onto her face and giving him more to deal with.

'Goodnight, you two. No talking once the light's out.' As if they'd take the slightest bit of notice. Cam tried to pull on a serious face but how could he when Marcus and Andrew looked so darned cute—make that cool—lying in their beds pre-tending to be ready for sleep. He knew the mo-ment he closed the bedroom door they'd roll over to face each other and yack their heads off for as long as he pretended not to know.

'Goodnight, Dad.' They both giggled.

How could Margaret have left them? He still couldn't get his head around that. Leave him? Yes, fine, if that was what she wanted. That particular pain had finally begun ebbing away. Shame the distrust couldn't do the same. But these guys deserved so much better from their mother. Bile rose in his throat.

It had been as if the bond that mothers presumably had from the moment they knew they were carrying a child had been missing in Margaret. Sure, the pregnancy had been unplanned. He should've seen the warning signs then. While he'd been ecstatic, she'd been upset. Unfortunately his belief that she'd get past that and fall in love with her babies when she held them for the first time hadn't eventuated. Instead, she'd focused more and more on her career until finally that had attracted her more than her children or her husband.

'Goodnight, Dad,' Marcus repeated. 'We want to go to sleep,' the little imp added, with eyes wide and the sheet already half off his skinny body.

'Dad?' Andrew sounded worried.

Three strides and he stood between the beds. Bending down, he scooped first Marcus then Andrew into his arms for a family hug. The scent of small boys filtered up his nose, warming him deep inside. 'I love you guys so much,' he whispered around the lump suddenly clogging his throat. How long since he'd last told them? These days he did more telling off than offering endearments. Something he really needed to work on.

Wriggle, wriggle. The boys slipped down and climbed back into bed. 'We love you, too.'

'Do you think Jenny's got anyone to love her?' asked Andrew.

Not if that desolation that tripped into her eyes at unexpected moments was anything to go by. 'I'm sure she has,' he lied. 'But it's not something you can ask her.'

'Why not?' The inevitable question hung between them all.

How to shut this down without upsetting the boys? 'When you don't know someone very well you can't ask a question like that. It's personal.' *That goes for you, too, Cam.* As Andrew's mouth opened Cam held up his hand. 'Wait. You don't want to make Jenny unhappy, and asking who loves her might make her very sad if there isn't anyone special.'

'We make her happy. She laughs with us.'

'You're right. She does that a lot when she's with you.' But not as much with him. Which might be a good thing. Too much laughter between them might lead to complications neither of them needed. He had his life mapped out: get these two through to adulthood as unscathed as possible. That meant focusing entirely on their needs and not his own.

Huh? What needs do I have anyway? I have food, warmth, shelter. I've a job that provides all those and helps towards keeping me sane. I'm the father of the greatest, coolest, funniest two kids ever born. It would be greedy to want more.

But when he stepped into the lounge and spied Jenny in the big old rocking chair Grandma had left him, the question repeated in his head. *Do I have other needs?* Loneliness surfaced, knocking the breath from his lungs. Strange because he was usually surrounded by people. But when was the last time he'd told anyone his dreams? Or made plans to go on a holiday with another adult to share everything with?

At the moment there was no one around to discuss decisions with about what to buy the boys for Christmas, or whether to apply for a partnership in the medical centre. Cam grimaced.

Some people would tell him he was lucky not having to take on board another person's ideas.

Glancing at Jenny, he wondered what it was about her that stirred up these pointless emotions and questions. Her chin rested on her gently rising and falling sternum, her eyes were firmly shut, those long, slim hands lying in her lap: the picture of abandonment. She'd finally succumbed to the exhaustion plaguing her all evening, which she'd been fighting with the tenacity of a bull terrier.

The sound of a small snore reached him. He grinned. She even sounded like a bull terrier. Kind of cute.

Smack. His palm banged his forehead. Cute? His boys were cute. Not this woman, who'd be gone within a day or two.

He might know next to nothing about Jenny Bostosk, but only a blind man wouldn't see that she moved on all the time. It was there in her eyes as they roved the horizon, in her short, sharp movements as if her body couldn't handle staying in one place for very long.

Which was just as well. Despite inviting Jenny into his home, he was not getting involved. It had

taken a long time to get over Margaret dump-
ing him. Even now he could feel the disbelief
that had slammed through him when she'd announced she was leaving him and the boys. So,
no, cute as Jenny was, he wasn't getting involved.

As his eyes scoped over her it dawned on him
that at this very moment she was completely, and
unusually, still. Her mind had obviously closed
up shop for the night. Bet that didn't happen
often.

Jenny needed to be in bed, not scrunched up
in a chair. He headed for the bedroom he'd made
hers for now and folded back the covers on the
bed, closed the curtains and turned on the bedside light. Returning to the living area, he drew
a deep, steadying breath and bent down to slide
his arms under her. Straightening his back, he
lifted her warm body and headed for the bedroom as fast as possible without disturbing her.
Having an antsy woman wake up in this situation would probably get his head beaten in.

But she didn't wake up. No, instead she snuggled in closer, causing his lungs to stall and his
muscles to tighten. All of them. Yeah, even that

one. Now, there was a surprise. It did still work. Even when it shouldn't.

Why did the spare bedroom have to be furthest from the lounge? His strides lengthened. Another of those cute little snores and warm air touched his chest through his shirt. Oh, hell. How was a man supposed to remain sane and responsible? How was his libido supposed to behave? There was a question he'd be wise not to dwell on. What was it about Jenny that had him waking up when he hadn't been the slightest bit interested in sex since before Margaret had left?

Almost dropping Jenny onto the bed, he dragged the covers over her, not bothering to remove any outer clothes—he didn't do stepping into lions' dens—and backed out of the room so fast he nearly tripped. Closing the door, he sagged against the wall and berated himself for a full five minutes. Thankfully swearing silently didn't count in the house rules. Not when the boys weren't in the same room as him anyway. If they had been he'd be coughing up buckets of cash in fines, not banking every spare dollar for their university fees in ten years' time.

Note to self: check how those investment funds

he'd started for the boys were doing. And tell his hormones to take a hike. Jenny was off limits.

The next morning Cam watched the boys place a plate of toast and a cup of tea on the bedside table with all the finesse of a calf wallowing in mud. 'Okay, say goodbye and go get your school bags, you two.'

Jenny gave each boy the benefit of her big smile. 'Breakfast in bed. How decadent. Thank you so much, Andrew. Thank you so much, Marcus.'

She never roped both boys into the one thanks or compliment. No, she singled each of them out. The boys' biggest gripe about being twins was that everyone spoke to them as though they were one unit. Everyone except Jenny. 'Are you a twin?'

Instantly the light in her eyes snapped off. Her hands clenched into fists before she slid them under the covers. Her bottom lip trembled.

Every swear word he could think of slammed into his brain. Now what had he started? It had seemed an innocuous question.

Marcus's eyes lit up. 'Are you like us? Where's

your sister? Or brother? Doesn't she want to be with you?'

Ice entered the room. Cam could feel his skin chilling and goosebumps rising. If he thought he'd seen desolation in her eyes yesterday, he didn't have a word to describe the shock, agony and the bewilderment darkening that summer green of her eyes to winter's darkest day.

'Out. Go get your bags and wait on the deck.' With a hand on their backs he nudged the boys towards the door, holding back the urge to rush them away before they added to his monumental blunder—whatever that was. 'Go. Now,' he growled, knowing this was his fault, not theirs, but needing them to do as he said quickly and quietly.

Maybe the frozen atmosphere of the bedroom had touched them too because they tiptoed away, glancing back over their shoulders with worried expressions on their faces. He gave a wave, hopefully reassuring, and turned back to the woman he'd obviously just knocked for a six.

'I apologise for putting my size elevens in my mouth, but you're so good with the boys the way you treat them as individuals and not as a double package that I figured you might know what it's like to be a twin. I never meant to upset you, but it seems I've done so in a big way.' Stop burbling on and on. But he needed to see that tension ease, to raise the tiniest of smiles on those now white lips. 'You are really, really good with my boys. It comes naturally to you.'

Her chest rose and fell sharply, quickly, continuously.

And finally he shut up except to say, 'Take a deep breath.'

It took a few attempts but eventually Jenny had her lungs under control. But not her eyes. They hadn't lightened, or met his gaze, or even blinked.

Leaning down, he tugged one of her hands free of the cover and wrapped it in both of his. It was cold. And shaking. Cam sat on the edge of the bed and held tight, his thumb rubbing gentle circles over the back of her hand. Slowly, slowly the quivering slowed, but didn't stop entirely.

Then Jenny pulled free and sat back against the pillows. 'Alison.'

Did he acknowledge her? Or would that start another episode of what he'd just witnessed? If he remained silent she might think he was deliberately ignoring her. He spoke as softly as he could manage. 'Your twin?'

Her head dipped. 'She died.'

He'd been getting to that. Her reaction had to have meant more than a sisterly fallout. 'I'm sorry. I can't begin to imagine how that must feel.'

'Stop apologising.'

'What?'

'You've been saying sorry ever since we met on the footpath. You don't need to.'

That had nothing to do with her sister. Probably her coping mechanism kicking into force. Jenny could relax about that. He wasn't about to jump in and ask the big questions about how, why, where. Hell, he wasn't going ask what she wanted sent from the bakery for her lunch. He'd bring something of his choice. 'Deal. No more apologies. Now drink your tea before it's totally cold.'

'Anyone ever tell you you're bossy?'

'The tw—' Swallow. 'Marcus and Andrew. All the time.' He handed her the cup and tried not to notice how much it shook in her two-handed grasp.

'Go. They'll be wondering why you're taking so long.' Colour was returning to her face at last.

Note to self: do not mention her twin sister at all ever again.

CHAPTER FIVE

JENNY WANTED TO throw up. No one in all the months she'd spent on the road had asked if she had a family, let alone if she was a twin.

She sipped the lukewarm tea and bit into the heavily buttered toast the boys had made her. Hopefully that would settle her stomach faster than holding her breath or plain old wishing the nausea away could.

If her foot hadn't been aching and throbbing and difficult to manoeuvre she'd have been tempted to catch a bus out of town, away from intrusive questions and prying eyes. Cam missed nothing. He'd seen each and every one of her emotions when he'd asked that question. He'd known instantly he'd made a big mistake, probably even had an inkling as to why. At least he hadn't gone all effusive on her. That would've caused her stomach to do what she was so far managing to prevent.

'Yes, I am a twin, who failed her other half. Yes, I totally get what it's like to have people put me and my twin into the same pigeonhole. We were born identical, shared a birth date and parents, had the same passion for hiking in the bush, but that's where the similarities ended.'

Just like Marcus and Andrew. Already she could see differences. They both liked playing cricket in the yard, but Marcus preferred bowling, concentrating with everything he had to bowl the perfect ball, while Andrew just wanted to slog the ball as far as possible with no thought to where it might land in relation to the lone fieldsman, being their dad, or to the house windows.

Their dad. Cam, or Cameron Roberts, as he'd introduced himself. An enigma. He loved his kids massively yet often seemed to be cross with them for very little reason. The guy needed to loosen up.

Ha! Like she could talk. Loose did not describe her at all. In any connotation. A wound-up rubber band was getting close. Wind it too tight and it might snap.

Not only had her life come to a crashing halt in

Havelock, having time on her hands was already forcing her to face things she'd had no intention of facing. There'd been some fun moments on this journey—like the beach at Whangamata where she and Alison had once given surfing a go. Neither of them had had the aptitude required to stay on a board long enough to ride a wave. This time she'd taken a surfing lesson, but had still bombed out. No doubt Alison had been laughing down at her.

Throwing the covers aside, she gingerly lowered her feet to the floor and stood up. Sucked in a breath and held onto it until the sharp jolt of pain faded.

After trying to juggle the cup and plate and use the crutches, she gave up, headed for the bathroom instead. She'd think of a way to take the cup and plate out to the kitchen later. Right now a shower was on the menu.

With Cam's usual thoughtfulness a large plastic bin liner and a roll of tape were on the sink top, and a stool had been placed strategically by the shower, with a towel folded neatly on top. He'd also placed her bathroom bag with her shampoo and conditioner beside the shower door.

She could get used to this. Cam was so caring. She wondered what had gone wrong with his marriage.

With her leg in the tightly taped bag, she hobbled under the jets of hot water and luxuriated in the heat pummelling her. Her body ached from top to toe from the thumping it had received when she'd hit the ground like a sack of spuds. Tipping her head back, she let the water saturate her hair then lathered in shampoo, at last returning the tangled mess to its silky texture. Now she felt half-human again. If only everything else needed to fix her problems came in a plastic bottle with a squeeze top.

Who knew that having a shower, getting dressed and making the bed could take so long? It was nearly lunchtime and Jenny stood at the kitchen bench with a cup of tea and pulled a face at the enticing sun-drenched deck. She wanted to be out there, drinking this, not standing here unable to move without her crutches.

Instead she turned to focus on the cork board next to the fridge. Covered in photos, school messages, party invitations and sports timetables, it gave her an insight into the Roberts family's day-to-day life. In a word—busy. And happy. In every photo one or all three of the males who lived in this house beamed out at the world.

'Big tick for you, Cam. You're obviously doing lots of things right with those two.'

Her heart squeezed. He was a great dad. His doctoring skills weren't shabby either. He'd been gentle and careful with her ankle, had asked the right questions. As for anything else, his long, lean body was pretty good, too, in great shape, if she dared to think about it.

Then there was that astute mind that picked up on vibes far too quickly. He didn't miss a trick. All in all, he added up to a very intriguing package. She hugged herself.

Don't go there, insisted a very familiar little voice in her head.

Finishing her tea, she carefully made her way out to the deck and dropped onto a wooden chair, breathed in the warmth and quiet.

Now what? She should've checked out that bookshelf to see if there was anything she could read. Even a mechanic's manual would be better than having nothing to distract her. Except she couldn't see Cam with his head under a bonnet. Though why not, she had no idea. Understanding men hadn't been one of her strong points.

'Hey, you're up and about.' Cam stepped onto the deck and stopped, his throat working overtime.

When the moment had stretched out too long and he obviously hadn't found his voice she asked, 'Has a bird left its calling card on my head?' Couldn't be food on her face. She hadn't eaten since her shower.

He swallowed hard. 'Yep, must've been a turkey from the size of the mess.'

Instinctively she ran her hand over her head and felt stupid for doing it, knowing he'd been teasing, or hiding something.

Cam held up two bulging paper bags. 'Lunch courtesy of the bakery.'

'Yum. I looked in their window on Saturday and everything looked very enticing.'

'Your hair is beautiful.' Then he disappeared inside to the kitchen.

Aha. That's what the throat movements had been about. He'd been stumped by her shocking red hair. No doubt the sun was highlighting all the tones and her head would be looking the colour of a cooked lobster. She called after him, 'I'm easily found in a crowd, that's for sure.'

'You don't like it?' Surprise registered on his face as he popped his head out of the kitchen window. 'Or is it that you don't like standing out in said crowd?'

As she'd said, too damned astute for his own good. 'I tried blonde once. Had lots more fun.'

A quick flick of those lips into a brief smile. 'Redheads don't have fun?' he asked.

Did he want to know if she was into fun? 'Definitely not. We're very serious people.' There was no stopping the grin splitting her mouth wide. Cam had some magic power that made her smile more than she had in for ever.

'But they drive fast sports cars.' He approached with plates, glasses of juice and the bags from the bakery. 'Bread rolls with smoked chicken and cranberry salad okay with you?'

'Just what I was about to ring out for.'

'So, how's that foot?'

She watched as he bit into his roll, noticing for the first time what perfect, white teeth he had.

So what? They're teeth. Everyone has them. But not everyone's teeth had her wondering how it would feel to be nibbled on her breasts or down her stomach.

'Jenny? A guy could be insulted with the number of times you go space tripping around him.'

Oh, I'm not insulting you, believe me. 'The foot's doing as well as expected. In other words, it's not ready to play football or do a tango. It does complain quite sharply at any sudden movement but, hey, we're still getting along.'

He shook his head at her. 'You are something, you know that?'

There really wasn't an answer to that. She bit into her lunch. 'How's your day going? Lots of patients?'

'The usual run of blood-pressure tabs, antihistamine scripts and general health checks. We're rarely rushed off our feet at this centre.' Was that longing in his eyes? 'But then there are the days when an emergency throws everything up in the air, and around here those tend to be messy.'

'You ever miss the busier practice in Wellington?'

'Do I?' He chewed thoughtfully. 'You know,

I've been too busy making sure the boys get established in their new life and are happy to stop and think about it. Two friends from med school and I started that practice. We were doing very well. Then one day Greg went for a run after work and had a massive coronary on the side of the road.'

'He didn't make it?' It was a reminder that other people had bad stuff happen to them and didn't run away.

'Yes, he did. But it was a huge wake-up call. Sometimes we seemed to be working more hours than we had in the ED as interns. We brought in more partners, but it was never the same. So the long answer is, no, I don't miss that particular practice. Though I now work so far at the other end of the stress scale I'm almost horizontal.'

'Yeah, right. That explains the shadows under your eyes.'

'I knew I'd forgotten something. Didn't put any make-up on this morning.'

Had his wife disliked the slow pace of Havelock? She wasn't asking. Instead she tried, 'Where do the boys go after school?' Maybe she could look after them until Cam got home.

'Amanda, the mother of one of their friends, takes them. She also takes their swimming lessons.'

Disappointment tugged at her. Of course he'd have everything organised. He hadn't been waiting for her to fall into his life to help out. 'Does she look after the boys in the school holidays, too?'

'No. They go to my parents on the farm. They love it out there so much it's always a battle to bring them home at the start of term.'

Parents. *Parents.* She missed her mum and dad. They understood what she was doing and why. Didn't they?

Cam stood up. 'Time I headed to Blenheim. Anything you want before I go?'

'No, I'm fine, thanks.' *Oh, for pity's sake, it won't hurt to ask a favour of him.* Swallow. 'Um, you couldn't get my tablet for me, could you?'

'Of course.' He looked puzzled that she had to ask. 'Where is it?'

'At the bottom of my bag.' Which meant he'd have to dig through all her clothes, including her underwear. If he even found her slightly attractive he'd only have to remember the boring, plain white knickers and bras he'd find there and he'd sober up fast.

Within minutes Cam had placed a bottle of iced water, some fruit and her tablet on the table beside her. He added a notepad with his email address at the top. 'In case you need anything.'

A hug wouldn't go astray. Gulp. What? A hug? Why?

Because she felt a wee bit lonely right now. Being forced to stay put so wasn't helping her cause. Instead she was doing stupid things, like considering emailing Mum and Dad and telling them where she was and how she'd managed to end up here when usually she only said enough for them to know she was still alive and kicking.

A deep breath and her shoulders went back. 'Hopefully, I won't be annoying you. Have a good afternoon, and I'll see you later.'

A finger lifted her chin and knowing brown eyes locked with hers. 'Believe me, an hour after we get home you'll be wishing for the peace and quiet again. School doesn't tire my boys. Instead, it winds them up even more.'

'They're like those battery bunnies from the TV ads.'

'Sometimes I wish I could just take out their batteries.' Cam's thumb slid across her chin before he dropped his hand to his side.

If she hadn't known better she'd have said it had been a caress. But she did know better. Cam had enough on his plate to deal with, without having the time or the need to be caressing her. 'Cam?' When she had his complete attention again she said, 'I really appreciate all you've done for me. Don't say you have to either, because you don't.'

'My lips are sealed.'

Her lips tipped up into a smile. 'Why did you bring me into your home?'

'My lips are sealed.'

Lips. Cam's lips. What would they feel like on hers? She watched as he stepped off the deck and headed for the front of the house without a backward glance. This whole scenario was alien to her, and yet it was tugging her in, wrapping around her, making her feel comfortable for brief moments of time. She tapped the tablet into life.

Hi Mum and Dad. That's great news about your trip to Sydney in the New Year.

This was where she'd normally sign off. But her fingers kept tapping the keys.

I am currently in Havelock. It's a quaint little town on the Pelorus Sound, famous for the green-lipped mussels grown in the sounds and packaged here at a small factory.

She stared out across the lawn to the hills beyond the Sound. According to her hiking book there were some walking tracks over there. Not that she'd been planning on doing any of those as she hadn't intended stopping here for longer than it took to eat lunch. But now she'd love the opportunity.

Mum, Dad, don't panic but I've broken my ankle. A silly little accident that has rendered me next to useless for a few days. The local doctor has kindly put me up until I'm ready to move on.

She chuckled. That made Cam sound old and avuncular.

He has two boys he's bringing up on his own. They're just adorable. Sigh. That's about it this time. Love you both heaps, Jenny.

She didn't hesitate, touched Send, and the longest email she'd written in a year headed off into cyberspace.

'Jenny, where are you?'

'We're home. Are you better?'

No way could she tell the twins apart by their voices. 'Hi, guys. I'm on the couch with a cat. Who does it belong to?' The black and white moggy had made itself very comfortable on her thighs an hour ago and she hadn't had the heart to send it packing.

'That's Socks. She lives at Mrs Warner's house, but Dad says we feed her more times.'

One boy appeared by the couch. Andrew? Fingers crossed she'd got it right, she said, 'Socks is quite heavy, isn't she? Andrew, can you lift her off so I can shift my legs?'

'Okay.'

Got the name right. Great. 'Thanks.'

'That cat's far too fat,' came an acerbic comment from the kitchen.

'Should I have put her outside, Cam?' Like that would be easy in her current situation.

'Good luck with that.' Cam strolled into view. 'How was your afternoon?'

'Excellent.' Joined the local theatre group and did a turn in the mussel-opening shed. 'It's unbelievably quiet here. I haven't done anything to help with dinner, I'm sorry.'

'You weren't expected to,' Cam glanced at her.

'We're having a barbecue.' Marcus bounced around the room until he found the TV remote.

'We always have barbecues,' Andrew explained in a bored tone.

Every time one boy spoke the other added his say. So like her and Alison it made her heart crunch. She'd stopped talking very much in those first months after Alison had left her because she'd found herself pausing and waiting for Alison to speak. Every time she hadn't, it had hurt all over again.

'Barbecuing is the easiest way to cook,' Cam muttered. 'Especially in summer.' Did he feel pressured about the meals he provided for his boys? They weren't exactly looking malnourished.

Licking her lips exaggeratedly, Jenny said,

'Barbecues are my favourite. Yummy food and no slaving over a hot stove.' Like she ever slaved over any kind of stove.

'Turn that TV off, Marcus. You haven't done your jobs yet. The washing needs bringing in.' Cam reached for the remote, tugged it from Marcus's hand. He raised his voice. 'Andrew, empty the dishwasher. Now. Bring your lunchboxes out to the kitchen first.'

Jenny grimaced. 'Can I do anything? Make a salad or peel some potatoes?' Sitting here while everyone else did the chores made her uncomfortable. She hadn't even noticed the washing on the line.

Cam was already returning to the kitchen. 'Stay where you are. We have a routine.' He turned and gave her a reluctant smile. 'For want of a better word.'

'I'd be in the way.' She got it. But tomorrow surely she'd be able to get around a bit better, and then she'd make herself useful.

'You would,' Cam agreed too easily.

The man looked so tired she wanted to insist on helping in one way or another, but she could see any interruption to his routine might be more of a hindrance than a help so she stroked the cat, which had returned to sprawl across her thighs, instead.

Marcus staggered in with an overladen washing basket and dropped it on the floor in the middle of the lounge.

'Push that over here and I can fold everything.' She nudged the cat aside and got a hiss for her effort.

'There's a novelty,' quipped the man himself, as he strode past to the glass doors opening on to the deck and that barbecue he was so fond of.

'Dad tips the clothes onto the table in the laundry and we take what we need when we want it.'

She had noticed the rumpled look worn by all three males in this house. Tomorrow she'd balance on her cast and iron some shirts.

'Give away all my secrets, why don't you?' Cam returned, ruffling his son's hair on the way past.

'I don't know anyone who likes ironing.' Except Alison had, driving her crazy with her fussiness when it had come to clothes. The memory tugged, sent a small wave of warmth through her. She held her breath, waited for the explosion of pain that followed such memories. It didn't happen. Now, there was a first. The day was going from weird to weirder. First she'd sent an email to Mum and Dad that had involved more than *hello, how are you.* Now she'd recalled something about Alison that hadn't sent her heart plummeting to her toes.

Marcus said, 'Dad says it's a waste of time.'

'Your dad's a busy man.' She didn't dare look around to see if Cam had heard. She'd bet her crutches he had. The man had ears everywhere. Putting a folded towel on the couch beside her, she reached into the basket for another one. 'I bet he does the most important things first, and then there's probably no time left for other jobs like ironing.' Sticking up for Cam now, eh? What was that about? Plain old empathy for a man who at times appeared overwhelmed with everything, that's what.

Despite her determination not to look for him, her gaze drifted sideways, searching, finding him standing in the middle of the kitchen, a plate of chops in one hand, a bottle of cooking oil in the other, and a bemused expression on his face.

She winked.

His bemusement intensified.

Astonishment made her mouth gape. Since when did she do winks? Never, ever. So she'd just proved what a moron she was, winking at the man who'd opened up his home to her. Winks and lechery were synonymous.

'You're dribbling.' Cam winked back.

A deep-bellied laugh rolled up her throat and spilled between them. A muscle-relaxing, heart-warming, pants-wetting-if-she-wasn't-careful laugh. Smudging her moist eyes with the back of her hand, she struggled to contain the merriment before she embarrassed herself.

Cam probably already thought she was nuts.

But when she finally looked at him he wore that smile, only this time it was wider, softer, more heart-melting than she'd seen before.

He said, 'You're nuts.'

See? 'I know.' And I haven't laughed like that for a year.

Caution, Jenny. Two days after meeting Cam you're lightening up on the stress levels, the gloom is lifting and you're starting to see the world in colour rather than a grey monotone. Be very careful. You could be in for a fall.

'You've got a message,' Marcus called from out on the deck. 'Want your tablet?'

'Yes, please.' She hadn't meant to leave it outside but when she'd realised what she'd done she'd been comfortably ensconced on the couch. Not that she ever got much in the way of emails these days. She had to stay in touch with people for that.

Mum had replied. No surprise there. She'd be worried about her accident, had probably booked a flight up to see her and make sure she was looking after herself. *I shouldn't have told them.*

Darling Jenny, sorry to read about your broken ankle. That can be debilitating. The doctor sounds nice, taking you in like that when he's probably already very busy. I expect that you're doing all you can to help him. Big hugs and lots of love, Mum.

Huh? Where were the questions? The demands to be careful? The details of the flight she was arriving on? Was this Mum's way of telling her it was time to stop moving and settle some-where?

'Who emailed you?' Marcus asked.

'My mother.' I think.

'You're lucky.' That sweet little face turned sad.

'Yes, I am. But you've got your dad and Andrew.' Neither replaced his mother. She got that. She had her parents but they didn't fill the gap left by Alison. 'They love you heaps.' She wouldn't say they'd always be there for Andrew because no one could predict that with abso-lute certainty. Look what had happened to her for believing she'd have Alison in her life for ever.

'I love my mum heaps.' Marcus stared at the floor, his hair falling across his eyes.

Reaching out, she pulled him near and sat him on the couch beside her, away from the washing. 'Of course you do. Mums are special.'

Still staring at the floor, he nodded slowly. 'Ours is.'

'So are dads and brothers.'

The nodding continued. 'Mine are the best.'

'See? You're very lucky. I bet they think you're the best, too.'

Finally Marcus raised his head and looked at her. 'Are you really a twin?'

CHAPTER SIX

CAM HELD HIS breath and waited for Jenny's withdrawal from Marcus. He should interrupt, tell Marcus to stop asking questions and get his homework, but something in the way Jenny didn't sink in on herself the way she had that morning made him pause. Besides, if he was being honest, he wanted to hear this too. Letting Marcus do his dirty work?

'Yes, I am. I…' She stopped, swallowed hard, then kept going. 'My parents had two girls. I'm the oldest. Alison was the bossy one, always telling me what to do.'

'I'm the bossy one *and* the oldest.'

True.

'Who's the brainiest?' she asked. Deflecting the twin subject?

Marcus's chest puffed out. 'I am.'

Not quite so true.

'No, he's not,' Andrew yelled across the

kitchen, where he was still slowly putting the clean dishes away, one piece of cutlery at a time. Why didn't he understand that if he just got on with the job it would be finished and he'd have more time for fun things? 'I got ninety-five for maths, you got eighty-one.'

Here came the war. Cam intervened, 'You're both intelligent in different subjects. Now, Marcus, set the table for dinner. Andrew, put four plates on the bench and get that dishwasher unpacked, will you? Before Christmas, if possible.'

Jenny stood up. 'I'll start hobbling towards the deck and hopefully I'll make it by dinnertime.' The smile she sent him was full of understanding and gratitude and warmth. She'd diverted the boys from asking more questions and he'd kept them diverted.

That's how it should be between parents, each backing the other subtly. Yet Jenny wasn't the boys' parent, didn't have kids of her own, and she'd managed to do that. Margaret had never done it, always looking for ways to come between him and the boys, finding an excuse for an argument. Was his main problem with Margaret that he'd chosen the wrong woman for himself? He'd loved her, deeply. Had he expected too much from that love? Something to think about when next he started getting serious about a woman. Huh. He'd better start thinking about that now then.

The knife fell from his hand to clatter into the sink. What the hell?

'You okay?' asked the woman responsible for his crazed brain.

'Sure.' Picking up the knife, he began slicing cucumber with a healthy regard for his fingers. Then he smiled.

Smiling used to come naturally. In fact, at one time he'd worn an almost permanent one. But that had been before everything had gone pear-shaped.

'Smells like burnt meat out here,' Jenny called, as she levered herself across to the barbecue. 'Nothing like a bit of crispy chop.' She started deftly flipping the chops over so the other sides could cook.

Great. Jenny's fault for distracting him so easily.

Note to self: keep focused around Jenny Bostock or more than the chops are going to get burned.

Another note to self: make those appointments for the boys' haircuts.

'Did you tell your parents about your fracture?' Cam asked, after he'd seen the boys to bed.

'Yes,' Jenny replied. 'They don't seem overly concerned, which is a relief, I guess.'

Jenny clicked shut the web page for the local bus company. There were plenty of choices for getting from Havelock to Blenheim if she chose to leave and find a motel. Maybe not tomorrow but the day after when she was bit more nimble.

'You making school lunches?' The guy hadn't stopped doing chores all evening.

Cam spread margarine on slices of bread. 'Yes. Every day except Friday when I let the kids buy their lunch from the bakery as a treat.'

'What other things need doing before you take a break?' He should be sitting down, watching TV or reading a book, talking to her over coffee, not moving from one job to the next. No wonder he looked exhausted all the time. Tomorrow she'd make sure to do some tidying up for him.

He glanced around the kitchen and shrugged. 'Think I'm nearly done. Did I mention you've got an appointment with Angus tomorrow? He called me, said I was the only contact he had for you. Hope that's all right. I kind of intimated I'm your GP for now.'

'What happened to calling my cell?' But he had been looking out for her yet again.

'I'd say Angus just phoned me without even considering checking your file. I made your appointment for the afternoon so that you can hitch a ride into Blenheim with me and I'll bring you home at the end of the day. You'll have to entertain yourself for a few hours after your appointment, that's all.'

'I can manage that.' Presumably there were cafés in Blenheim. Or she could find that motel she should be moving into. 'Thanks,' she added, as an afterthought. Cam had gone out of his way to help her and she'd neglected to be appreciative. 'Again, you've been more than helpful. I do appreciate it.'

'Even having me as your GP?' He gave her a glance that from anyone else would've been cheeky. With Cam she couldn't tell.

'Beggars can't be choosers.' She smiled. Amazing how easy it was to smile with him. Why wouldn't it be? He was a ten on the sexy scale. Any female with half a brain would be smiling at him.

'Where is your GP? Which town?' Cam spoke tentatively, as though afraid she'd tell him to mind his own business.

Which she normally would do. But what the heck? It wasn't as though she'd be giving anything major away if she answered. 'Dunedin. That's where I grew up and went to med school.'

'Your folks still live there?'

'Yes. They'll never leave, say there's no place like it. They're not wrong about that, but whether it's the best place in the country, I'm not so sure. The weather's the pits, for starters.' Too many freezing cold days with snow and ice interfering with plans.

'Where would you choose?' He snapped off a length of plastic wrap for the lunches.

'I have no idea. My last job was in Auckland but I can't say I liked that city much. Too big and sprawling for me.'

'Got a favourite place?'

'I used to have a fixation with mountains. Not as a place to live, though. The sea is appealing, though I've never lived on the waterfront.'

'What changed your mind about the mountains?'

So much for keeping this light. She should've kept her mouth firmly shut. 'I've done a lot of hiking, seen more of the back country than most people, and think it's time to find another interest.' A safer one. Mum and Dad didn't need to lose their other daughter.

It was apparent in his steady, sympathetic gaze and the way his smile slowly slid off those tempting lips that Cam knew she'd winged that answer. Thankfully he let it go. 'Feel like a coffee?'

'Can I have tea instead? Coffee will keep me awake half the night.'

'Sure, though I doubt anything's going to stop you from sleeping when you finally make it to bed. You've got serious bags under your eyes.'

'Charming.' Any time he mentioned her going to bed her tummy did a little skip. This time, as an added extra, her mouth dried. Bed and Cam in the same sentence were obviously too much to get her head around. He was hot. Scorching hot. But not a reason to get in a dither about. Oh, so her libido was meant to disappear for ever, was it? Was she not allowed to wake up and start looking at men again? It's not as though she was planning a long-term relationship with Cam. If anything—and that was a big if—she'd only want a fling. A very short one at that because she wouldn't be staying past Wednesday. A fling implied enjoying herself, something she wasn't ready for.

Cam said, 'I trained at Otago Med School, too. But I'd have been four, five, years ahead of you.'

She'd have remembered him. 'I'm thirty-one, started at university when I was eighteen.'

'Definitely long gone before you started.'

'So you're a geriatric?' He'd be about six years older than her, she reckoned.

'Definitely. Milk in your tea?'

Nodding, she asked, 'So why Wellington for your practice?'

Handing her the mug of tea, he sank into an armchair with his coffee. 'I went to boarding school there.'

'Why boarding school?'

'My parents have been farming in the sounds for forty-odd years. Mum home-schooled us until we were ready for high school.'

'How'd that go for you?'

'Loved it. I came home every opportunity, but being in the city was exciting, too.'

'It must've been poles apart from the life you grew up with.'

'Absolutely.' He blew on his coffee. Looked around the room, brought his gaze back to her. 'On Saturday you said you were travelling to Blenheim. Any particular reason?'

Time to drink up the tea and head to that bed he'd mentioned. This time her libido remained quiet. 'No, not really.'

He didn't look away or say a word. Just waited for an explanation. It would be hard to hide anything from him. But she didn't owe him an explanation.

The silence grew, not awkward but none too comfortable either. Gingerly sipping her tea, she thought about being here, doing something as ordinary as drinking tea and idly talking about life. How strange to have someone asking about what she did and where she did it. These past months the few people she'd crossed paths with hadn't even known she was a doctor. 'I haven't worked for a while. Taking a road trip instead.' And that's all I'm saying.

'A long road trip?'

'I'm nearly done.' The end was in sight. Except now she had no idea what she was going to do about getting to Kahurangi. Her foot wouldn't be in any fit state for driving, and there was no other way to get there. Buses went past but being dumped in the middle of nowhere without means of shelter and food wasn't viable. As for climbing to the accident site—forget it. Impossible.

'Jenny?' Cam called softly. 'If there's anything else I can do you'll tell me, won't you?'

His eyes looked as startled as hers felt, indicating that had come out of the blue as much for him as it had for her. Her eyes widened and a smile stretched her mouth. 'You've already done heaps. I'll be heading away, out of your hair, as soon as possible.' Then disappointment rocked her. She didn't want to move on. Not yet, not until she'd learned more about Cam. But staying would be unfair. He had more than enough to contend with, without adding her woes to his list.

'Will you eventually go back to working in an ED? Or do you want to change specialties?' At least he hadn't out and out asked why she'd given up medicine.

'Emergency medicine's always been my passion, and it's hard to imagine learning another specialty.' Even she could hear her voice dwindling away, getting quieter and quieter. Not wanting to face any more questions about any of this, she hauled herself upright and scooped up the crutches. 'Think I'll hit the sack.'

Cam's eyes widened, but thankfully he kept whatever had crossed his mind to himself. Instead, after a drawn-out moment he shocked her with, 'They're always looking for emergency specialists at Wairau.'

Bang. She was on her butt again and sucking in a pain-filled breath as her ankle protested at the sudden movement. 'I don't think so,' she finally spluttered.

He shrugged as if it was no big deal. Which it wasn't to him. 'Fine. Just letting you know. In case you were contemplating staying around.'

Thanks, but, no, thanks. It was one thing to feel disappointment at the thought of leaving, quite another to have Cam make it sound possible to stay. 'I'll keep it in mind.'

'Here, let me help you up.' Cam stood in front of her, hand extended. 'That was some thump you took just then.'

'Not sure what happened.' Yeah, right.

'I upset you again.' Contrition blinked out at her from those disturbing eyes.

Shaking her head from side to side, she said, 'Not your fault. Anyone would make the same suggestion given the situation.' Because they had no idea what she was up against. Placing her hand in his, the instant heat that warmed her had her making to tug away, except Cam closed his fingers around hers and held tight, pulling her to her feet.

Raising her gaze to meet his, she sucked in a breath at the need and loneliness and understanding she saw. Just as suddenly she wanted something from him too. Wanted friendship, closeness—wanted that fling she'd thought about earlier. It was there for the taking. She could see Cam's need in his eyes, feel it in his raised pulse as he held her hand, smell it in the thick air hanging between them.

Like a chrysalis slowly opening so that what lay inside could spread its wings and try to soar, it was as though her life was starting over. That she was being given a second chance. Her body swayed closer to his.

She didn't deserve a second chance. She pulled back.

Cam continued to watch her as he leaned close again. She only had to lift ever so slightly on her toes and her lips would be on his. And then she'd know what it was like to kiss Cam, to taste him.

Tugging her gaze away from that beautiful face looking down at her, she glanced around the room. Looking for? Approval? Condemnation? Toy trucks and a helicopter and a plane were stacked messily in one corner. *Toys, Jenny, toys.* Children lived here, with this man. They had first dibs on Cam, not her. She didn't have any dibs. What had she been thinking? Maybe she *had* hit her head when she'd fallen. She'd sure been acting strange ever since.

Jerking her hand free, Jenny hobbled sideways around Cam. 'Sorry,' she muttered. 'I need to get some sleep.' Then she might be able to put these out-of-left-field thoughts about Cam to rest.

Silently he handed her the crutches, watched as she tucked them under her arms. His face gave nothing away. That need she'd seen moments earlier had been banished. Thank goodness. It was hard enough controlling her own wayward reaction, without seeing the same staring back at her from the man who'd sent her libido into a tango in the first place.

'Goodnight, Jenny.'

A sharp nod, a curt 'Goodnight' and she clomped down the hall to the bedroom she used.

Now she really did have to find somewhere else to stay until she could get around more easily. Staying here any longer wasn't fair on Cam—or herself.

Tomorrow you're going with Cam to Blenheim to see your surgeon. You could spend those spare hours afterwards ringing around motels, enquiring about a suitable unit.

She could. It was the perfect solution. So why didn't she feel ecstatic? Why wasn't she hopping up and down with glee to know the end of staying here and being a pain in the butt for Cam was in sight?

She didn't want to leave. She liked it here, enjoyed the boys, nearly as much as their father. She felt comfortable, was even relaxing enough to start communicating more with her mum and dad.

All the more reason to be moving on. Whether she wanted to or not was irrelevant. Cam Roberts certainly didn't need the added distraction of her suddenly wide-eyed, ready-to-roll libido coming between them.

Knock, knock.

She spun round. The crutches slipped, tangled around her legs and tipped her onto the bed. Pain sliced through her ankle, ripped up her leg, sent nausea crawling up her throat. She let out a strangled cry.

'Hey, careful.' Cam pushed open the door and was instantly at her side, reaching down to remove the crutches. 'I'm sorry. I thought you'd hear me coming along the hall. I wasn't trying to be quiet.'

Deep breaths, in one two, out one two. In, out. Slowly, slowly the pain ebbed away, leaving her feeling drained. 'Goes to show I'm not improving as fast as I thought,' she finally gasped out.

Cam knelt down and gently straightened her leg. 'As fast as you'd like, you mean.'

'I guess.'

'Are you always so impatient?' Straightening up, he lifted her to stand on the good foot and quickly whipped back the bed covers before lowering her onto the bed.

'Me? Impatient? Only when I need to get something done.' Great, now she was in bed, fully dressed and her body craving to relax back into the mattress. But she was damned if she'd undress while Cam was still in the room. Not after that searing moment back in the lounge.

Cam obviously had other ideas. He pulled the oversized T-shirt she slept in from under the pillow and handed it to her. 'You have something you want to do urgently? Some place you need to be? Or are you in a hurry to leave us?'

'All of the above.' That wasn't a fib.

He crossed to close the curtains, tossing a question over his shoulder. 'What's so important you can't give that fracture a couple of days to start mending?'

'I hate being a nuisance.' Avoid the big questions. Makes life far easier. 'My ankle can heal just as well in a motel as it can hanging out on your deck.'

He turned back to face her. 'Sounds kind of lonely to me.' There was disappointment and something a bit like hurt in that steady gaze locked on her. 'But I guess being stuck with two highly energetic kids and their grumpy father could be worse for someone who obviously prefers her own company.'

Her heart rolled over. 'You're not grumpy.' Well, not often. 'Anyway, I'm not stuck.' Her gaze dropped from that devastatingly attractive face to her encased ankle. 'Not much.' Maybe tomorrow Angus would organise a new, stronger cast for her ankle so she could get around more easily, take in the sights of Havelock the day after tomorrow. Though what would she do for the rest of the day, when she'd finished perusing the few shops?

'You're not used to stopping in one place for any length of time, are you? Especially somewhere as small as Havelock?'

See? She knew he could read her like an open

book. How had he learned to do that? 'That depends what I stop for.'

Again disappointment filtered through his eyes. 'Get some sleep, Jenny. Your eyes are bugging with exhaustion.'

'Bugging now? You need practice on complimenting a woman.'

Heat singed his cheeks but he didn't look away. 'I'll look on line for a book that might give me some pointers.' There was that little smile, albeit a tad reluctant.

That smile warmed her in places she'd been cold all year. That smile came with a danger warning. She really needed to be moving on—fast. Yet knowing and doing seemed poles apart right at this moment.

Not that she'd be falling into a deep sleep easily. Too much going on inside her head for that to happen. Cam had rattled her in more ways than one and she needed to work her way through everything so she'd wake up refreshed and ready to stride ahead and leave him behind—metaphorically if not physically.

But the next thing she was aware of was the sound of the boys calling each other names as they ran down the hall. Glancing around the room, she noted the sunlight at the gap in the curtains where Cam hadn't quite made them meet.

She'd overslept. Hardly unusual. Waking up early was not her thing. Nothing was worth rushing out of bed for. What about a glimpse of Cam's mouth-watering, muscular body to start her day off? What about getting her head on straight? Leaving Cam behind should be the plan. Tomorrow would do for that.

Sitting up straight, Jenny raised her arms over her head to stretch high. She felt good. When she tentatively wriggled her toes even her damaged foot seemed a lot happier this morning. Perhaps some of the swelling had gone down.

Tossing the covers aside, she clambered out of bed and got a shaft of pain for her efforts. Had she spoken too soon? She waited for the throbbing to calm down before limping across to pull open the curtains fully.

There was a light knock on her door. 'Jenny, you awake?' Cam called softly.

'Of course I am.'

The door opened wide and Cam stepped in,

taking up all the breathable air at the same time. 'How are you this morning? Those eyes don't appear so bugged.' He stood watching her hop across the room in a T-shirt that barely covered her bottom.

She replied, 'I'm good. Really good.'

Cam gave an affirmative nod in her direction, but his gaze didn't lift to her face. He thought she was good? In what way? The tip of his tongue appeared between his lips, sending her heart rate skittering all over the show.

'Was there something you wanted to ask me?' she croaked. There were a few things she'd like him to ask, but that wasn't going to happen.

He shook his head. 'No, nothing.'

'Then I'll see you at lunchtime?' she asked.

'Yes. You'll have to get your own breakfast. I did poke my head in an hour ago to see what you might like but you were comatose, and now I'm running late.'

'No problem.' Cam had peeked in on her and she hadn't been aware? Running her hand over her mussed hair, she winced. Just as well. No doubt she looked like a train wreck.

Cam's eyes still seemed drawn to the bottom of her T-shirt.

She dropped onto the bed and tugged the covers over her legs. 'If you're late, hadn't you better get moving?'

He blinked as colour reddened his cheeks. 'You're right.' Turning his head, he called, 'Come on, boys. Chop, chop. Pack your bags, put your sandals on.'

'Chop, chop.'

'Chop, chop,' the twins mimicked as they charged along the hall.

Jenny could no longer hold back a smile. 'I remember that. Alison and I repeating everything Mum said. Boy, did we wind her up at times, especially if she was in a hurry or in a bad mood.'

'I'm not in a bad mood,' Cam growled.

'Of course not.' Her smile widened.

His scowl deepened. 'Think I prefer it when you're asleep.' He followed his sons, stomping along the hall.

Laughter bubbled up. 'Temper, temper,' she said, but not so loud that he'd hear. She did need a ride into Blenheim later.

Temper, temper, had been her and Alison's favourite taunt with Mum. They had been naughty at times. But always jointly, each egging the other on. Had Mum looked as tired as Cam did? She had no idea. Though there had been that time that Dad had left them with the neighbour they hadn't liked so he could take Mum out to a fancy restaurant for dinner—to give her a break from them.

Mum and Dad. They'd been the greatest parents any two girls could have wished for. Yeah, and look how she'd treated them these past months—almost ignoring them. Yet they were still so patient with her, waiting for her to work through her grief in her own way, while dealing with their own at the same time.

Where was her tablet?

She found it in the lounge and after making a cup of tea and toasting a slice of multigrain bread she began an email.

Dear Mum and Dad.

It's kind of fun being in this household. Marcus and Andrew remind me so much of the mischief Alison and I got up to. Cam, their father, looks exhausted all the time. I guess we did that to you, too.

I'm going for my check-up with the surgeon today and will have to wait in Blenheim for a ride home with Cam.

She was calling this place home now? What would Cam think of that? Probably pack her bag and put it out on the pavement at the bus stop.

Not sure when I'll be ready to leave here. The car's parked up in the garage here and Cam says I can leave it for as long as I want. Will keep you posted on my next moves.
Loads of love, Jenny.

Tapping the 'send' icon, she shook her head, admitting it felt good to finally have something to say without wondering if mentioning Alison's name would hurt them, or if not mentioning her sister hurt them even more.

Marcus and his skateboard had a lot to answer for. All she had to figure out was whether it was a good or bad thing. Draining the cup of tea she'd all but forgotten, she pushed to her feet. Time for a shower and an end to thinking. Thinking was highly overrated.

In the bathroom Cam had again set up everything for her. Even the rubbish sack was a new one. That man was too thoughtful for his own good. She smiled. But not for hers.

Was Cam like this with everyone? Or just her?

Did he feel attracted to her? Like she did to him?

No point in denying it—she found him physically exciting. And there was more—that thoughtfulness was sexy, as was his tenderness, determination to do the best for his boys, and just about everything about him. This was bad. And exciting.

CHAPTER SEVEN

'WHAT CAN I SMELL?' Cam's nose wrinkled as he sniffed an acrid burnt odour the moment he stepped inside his house. It had been a particularly gruelling day. Lack of sleep over the previous nights while Jenny had tripped through his head had only made it harder to deal with Roy Franks's unwillingness to listen. He'd told the man he'd die if he didn't have the open heart surgery he was booked in for next week, but Roy was still refusing. Sure, the man was scared witless. Who wouldn't be? But the operation had to be better than the alternative.

In the kitchen, standing behind the island, Jenny stared at him, embarrassment written all over her pretty face. Her eyes flicked to him and away again. 'How hard can it be to boil rice? Millions of people cook it every day. They don't burn it to the bottom of the pot, do they?'

Burnt rice? What was she up to now? 'Why do

you want rice?' He had new season's potatoes ready to cook with mint picked from Mrs Warner's garden that morning. Lamb patties were on a plate covered with a paper towel in the fridge, all ready for the barbecue. All he had to do was toss together a salad.

Jenny glared at him. 'I'm cooking dinner for you. Thought I could give you a break since you've been so good to me. Guess I got that wrong.' Her glare turned woeful as she glanced at a recipe book on the counter. Asian meals.

She needed a recipe book to cook rice? Guess the disaster facing him answered that in the affirmative. 'Cooking not your strong point?' Despite the mess facing him, he couldn't help grinning at her.

Jenny winced. 'Not really.'

He saw the pot in the sink filled with water, presumably to soak off the layer of blackened rice he could see on the bottom. The pot looked ruined. Turning, he nodded in the direction of a serving dish on top of the stove containing something resembling the cat's biscuits when she regurgitated them on the floor. 'What's that?'

'Chicken chasseur.' Jenny glared at the dish,

and continued in a woeful tone, 'At least, that's what it's meant to be but it looks nothing like the picture on the packet.'

'Packet?' Where was her beautiful smile?

'Yes. One of those add-water-and-cook things.' Heat was creeping into her usually pale cheeks.

'Were the instructions in Swahili?'

'So I'm not the world's greatest cook, all right? But I wanted to help out instead of sitting on my behind and being waited on hand and foot.' Jenny locked eyes with his. 'I've managed to empty the dishwasher and bring in the washing without incident.' Then she turned towards the fridge.

Reaching out, he caught her elbow and stopped her. 'Thanks. I do appreciate everything.'

Jenny didn't look at him now so he used his finger under her chin to lift her head and caught his breath at the tears threatening to spill down her face. 'Hey, I meant it. Truly.'

He should step away right this minute but for the life of him he couldn't. Those big beautiful summer eyes were bigger, greener and more beautiful, enhanced by the moisture she was trying to ignore. Big pools that he could easily drown in. Was drowning in.

'Then you won't mind me making the salad.' Jenny pulled back and reached to open the fridge. Lifting the vegetable bin, she once again averted her eyes.

Taking the bin from her hands, he smiled again. This woman had him relaxing even when she'd turned his kitchen into a tip. 'No insult, but I'll make the salad. But, first, why don't we have a glass of wine on the deck?' She did drink wine, didn't she? He hadn't offered before now because she'd been taking painkillers, but that morning she'd announced she'd stopped. Going to tough it out, she'd said, drugs being something she preferred not to take. Her new, lighter cast probably helped too.

'You're offering me a consolation prize?'

'No, you'd be giving me some adult time.' Something he sorely missed whenever he thought about it, which was why he didn't waste time mulling it over. Usually he was so busy just doing what had to be done to keep his head above water that he didn't consider what he might be missing out on, and yet now with Jenny in his house there were many things popping into his mind that hadn't been around for a long, long time. 'Cabernet sauvignon or sauvignon blanc?'

'Sav blanc, thank you. Want some cheese and crackers with that? There's a block of Havarti in the fridge. I only have to open two packets and put them on a plate.' The tears had retreated, and that sweet mouth was starting to curl upwards.

'Can't go too wrong with that.' He found her a serving plate then poured their drinks, white for her, red for him. 'You've chosen one of my favourite cheeses.'

'So the woman in the little café shop told me.'

She'd gone to the trouble of asking? Wow. That showed her caring side. 'So what do you think of our little town?' She was still here, wasn't she?

'Would quaint be insulting?'

'Depends who you're talking to.' Mrs Warner would agree. Others would hate her for uttering such a word. He led the way outside and pulled out a chair for her. Watching her progress, it was obvious she'd well and truly got the hang of the crutches. 'Delia, my nurse, said she'd seen you out walking when she went to the bakery to buy us all morning tea.'

'I suppose there aren't too many people hobbling around Havelock with one foot in a cast.' She eased herself down onto the chair and slid back before laying the crutches on the floor under the table out of the way.

'You got it.'

'There are some interesting little shops, but how do they survive? It's not exactly downtown Auckland.'

Not even central Blenheim. 'There's a small but steady stream of tourists over the summer months, and in winter some of the shop owners close up and others slog it out.'

'This Mrs Warner? Your neighbour? I haven't seen her yet.'

'She's away visiting family for a fortnight.' Which was why she hadn't done his grocery shopping. Knucklehead that he was, he'd forgotten all about that until he'd been heading to Wairau Hospital to con Jenny into coming home with them.

He watched Jenny sipping the wine, her lips delicate against the glass, her throat moving as she swallowed. His gut tightened, as did muscles lower down. Steady. This fascination was getting out of hand. *So look away. Can't.*

'That turkey been flying over my head again?' she asked.

'No. I'm liking what I see, that's all.' That's all? That's a lot. Women hadn't featured in his life since Margaret and yet a few days of having Jenny around and he felt as though he was coming alive. Hadn't known he'd been half-dead until this week.

'Your compliments are improving.' She smiled at him, a full-blown, breath-shortening smile that rocked him.

Oh, boy. He was so lost. Standing up, he said, 'I'll turn the barbecue on,' and immediately tripped over his own feet, managing to slosh wine down the front of his trousers. Great, now he had a kitchen and trousers to clean up. Not to mention the stirrings of arousal.

'Go change and bring me those pants. I do know something about removing stains. They won't end up looking like that chasseur, I promise.' Her smile turned to a cheeky grin. 'And watch where you're going this time.'

He spun around, took long, fast steps away

from her. If she saw the bulge at the front of his pants she'd call the harassment police. Since when did his lack of a sex life matter so much? Why had his body leapt to life over Jenny?

Because she's beautiful and sexy, and pulls me in with those amazing eyes.

Note to self: stay away from that enticing smile. It's too distracting. Stay away from those eyes. They're dangerous.

And as he headed inside he saw the boys sprawled across the floor in front of the TV.

Second note to self: make those blasted appointments for haircuts.

Jenny worked the stain out and rinsed the trousers. Hard not to envisage the way this fabric had sat over that firm butt just minutes ago. Thankfully Cam had disappeared inside to remove them. Actually getting an eyeful of his rear view, or the front one, for that matter, if he'd shucked the trousers off outside might've given her palpitations.

Hobbling outside, she hung them on the line. The temperature hovered around twenty so with a bit of luck they'd be dry by the morning.

Her gaze cruised the yard. Cam didn't have much of a garden. Guess he didn't have the time. Or maybe he didn't have the inclination.

There was something she'd learned from Mum: how to grow flowers. Nothing more rewarding than seeing beds of brightly coloured freesias, daisies, roses, peonies springing to life over the warm months. To pick a handful of flowers she'd grown and place it in a vase on the table had always made her happy.

Cam's talent seemed to be in mowing the lawn in a circle, starting at the outside and working his way into the centre, by the looks of it. Lines from the last cut were still apparent. She could picture him striding out fast, aiming to get the job done before tackling the next chore. He never seemed to stop, always had more than enough to do. Though tonight he had sat down with a wine. Yeah, look how that had quickly turned to a mess.

At the end of the lawn a swing set looked neglected and unused. She shuffled onto the seat and with her good foot pushed back. When had been the last time she'd been on a swing? With Alison at the park in Surfers Paradise when

Mum and Dad had taken them there for a holiday as teenagers. They'd been trying to impress some guys who'd been hanging around and Alison had reckoned they'd look cute on the swings. It had been a big fail.

Another Alison memory and she wasn't shaking with despair. Must be something in the Havelock air for her to be feeling more relaxed about everything that had happened. Would she ever come to terms with her grief? No, that would be expecting too much. Take one small step at a time. 'You lost your mojo in a big way. Don't rush trying to find it again.'

'Where did you lose your mojo?' asked one of the twins from behind her.

'What's a mojo?' asked the other.

'Can we help you find it?'

Stopping the swing, she turned to look at the boys. She hadn't realised she'd been talking out loud until they'd spoken up. 'Mojo is me, who I am, where I came from and where I'm going. The drive that keeps me going.'

Two blank faces stared at her.

'I lost it a year ago and now I want to find it so

I can be happy again.' Would they understand that better?

'We can help you.'

They already were. The boys, along with Cam, treated her so normally that she had started coming alive again. 'Thank you.'

'If we help you—'

'Will you help us find something?' Andrew finished the question Marcus had started.

'Sure. What have you lost?' She already knew Andrew was in trouble with Cam for losing a sports shoe this week.

'Our mother. We can't find her anywhere.'

Oh, no. She'd well and truly walked into that one. These poor little guys looked and sounded distraught. Her heart squeezed painfully for them, her stomach sunk in on itself. 'I…' What did she say? Anything that came to mind would only hurt them more. She didn't know the circumstances, and this so wasn't her place. Except they were watching her, each with a plea in his eyes that would be impossible to deny.

'We only want to see her and give her a hug.' Andrew looked ready to burst into tears.

Jenny shoved off the swing and snatched both

boys into her arms and held them tight. Not the hug they were wanting but she couldn't not hold them. They trembled against her, clinging to her as if for dear life. 'I know you do. I'd love to hug my sister.'

But that was different. Alison had gone. These boys' mother had to be somewhere. How could the woman leave her sons? Unbelievable. There was nothing that would be a good enough reason.

She sensed Cam's presence a second before his arms went around their little group, like an outer wrapping. His hand on her shoulder was warm and gave her the courage to raise her head and look directly at him.

'Thank you,' he mouthed. His eyes glittered as pain and anger and despair battled for supremacy in his lean face. So he'd heard what the boys had said. How often had he had to deal with this? How did he cope? Then he dropped a kiss on each boy's head and stood up slowly, unravelling himself and then the boys from around her.

What about me? Can I have a kiss too?

What she got was, 'Here, I'll give you a hand getting up.'

She'd forgotten about her ankle, but the moment Cam mentioned it she placed her hand in his and let him pull her gently upright, then leaned against him for a moment before he led her back to the deck to sit down.

'Where's your twin?' one of the boys asked, as he joined them on the deck.

Her shoulders drooped. What should she say? Would the boys think their mother had died too if she told them the truth? But she couldn't lie to them. That wouldn't help anyone. Looking at Cam for guidance, she found sympathy and saw a small nod. After a sip of wine she drew a deep breath and told them as simply as possible.

'My sister had an accident. We were mountain climbing and the track we were on gave out from under us. We fell over the cliff all the way to the bottom. Alison hit her head on a boulder.' The glass twirled back and forth in her fingers. 'She died there. I miss her heaps.'

Andrew clambered onto the bench to sit on her left side. Marcus did the same on her right. Cam looked astonished. Which was nothing to what she was feeling.

'That's sad. I'd miss Andrew if that happened

to us.' Marcus snuggled closer. 'He's my best friend as well as my brother.'

Sniff. 'Yes, that's how it is for twins.' Another sip of the wine. 'You know, we're luckier than everyone else because we're twins. No one else has a special person that close to them.'

Marcus pulled back to stare up at her. 'Was Alison as pretty as you?'

'You are a right little charmer, aren't you?' Her smile wavered. 'Alison looked just like me.'

'How did people know who was Alison—'

'And who was you?'

Oh, boy, this wasn't getting any easier. 'Alison was always smiling. She was very funny and made everyone laugh.' Whereas I was the serious one. Except when I was with my sister.

Cam refilled her wine glass, even though she'd barely touched it. 'Here, enjoy that.' He handed it over. 'Marcus, Andrew, let's give Jenny a break now. Dinner will be ready soon so how about you empty your schoolbags and put the lunchboxes on the bench?'

'Thanks.' Jenny watched them scurry to do what they'd been asked. 'Not sure where in the kitchen they can put anything. I did spread out a bit.'

'A bit?' Cam choked on his wine. She patted his back hard until he held a hand up and drew a deep breath. 'If I didn't know better I'd say a tornado had passed through the kitchen.'

'You do tend to exaggerate.' Reluctantly she withdrew her hand, trailing it across his shoulder blade and upper arm. The warmth Cam radiated hit her deep inside. A rare warmth from touching another human being. That joint hug of Cam's had been the first in a long time.

'Who? Me?' His smile was tight, his breathing a little rapid.

Because of her hand on him? Oh, great. Now what had she done? Did he fancy her? More to the point, did she want him to fancy her? 'Yes, you.' Now which question was she answering? Total confusion reigned in her head and she looked away.

Cam did that finger under her chin thing and tipped her head up and sideways so she couldn't avoid looking into his eyes. 'Thank you for telling the boys your story. I know it's very different from their mother walking away, but they seem to have picked up on something with you, and being twins that's helping them.'

'It must be difficult for you every time they think they've seen their mother. Is that what happened on Saturday? One of them said something about seeing her.'

'You got it in one.' His hands clenched and his body tensed. 'Some days I could strangle her for hurting them. All Marcus and Andrew ever asked for was to be loved. What's so wrong with that?' Spinning on the balls of his feet, he stared across the lawn, seeing who knew what.

'How long has she been gone?' Would he tell her to mind her own business?

'Two years and five weeks.' The desolation in his voice rolled her heart. She wanted to wrap her arms around him in a return hug, to take away that misery, but she couldn't move. What if he rejected her gesture?

Why would he? Why wouldn't he? They hardly knew each other, despite the fact she'd told him very briefly, via the twins, about Alison—something she never told anyone.

Did he still love his wife? Did he look for her in shops, too? Probably, if that far-away gaze was an indicator. Which meant she had no right feeling anything about him other than that he was a nice guy being very kind to her. Time to move on in case she started feeling something stronger for him. She'd talk about that after dinner when the boys were tucked up in bed. Tomorrow she'd head to a motel in Blenheim.

Dinner. The barbecue had waves of heat coming off it. 'Cam, I think you need to turn the barbecue off for a while or we're going to be eating charcoal.' Clomping inside, she retrieved that vegetable bin he'd taken off her earlier. She'd make the salad before cleaning up the mess she'd created.

It took for ever to wipe down all the surfaces, get that pot looking more or less how it used to, and make a salad.

By the time they'd all eaten and the dishes had been rinsed and stacked in the dishwasher Jenny was ready to take the weight off her foot.

Cam sat at his computer. 'Monthly health department requirements,' he muttered over his shoulder in answer to her query about why he was still working.

'You don't have an office person to deal with

that?' Filling the kettle, she flicked it on and found the teabags. 'You want tea?'

'Please. We do have office staff but the partners insist all of us check the figures pertaining to our own work. Pain in the backside at times.' Cam leaned closer to the screen. 'Especially when my receptionist never makes mistakes.'

'You'll have to come and get your tea. I'm done with cleaning up my messes,' she quipped, as she placed a plate of chocolate-chip cookies by his mug, 'I'd have baked a cake but you're out of flour.'

'You got these at the bakery.'

'Hope you like them.'

'They're the best. Don't tell the boys you bought some or they'll be gone.'

Guilt flared for leaving them out of the treat. 'Should I have given them one before they went to bed?'

'No. They'll probably get some on Friday when they buy their lunch.'

'You're not averse to a treat, then?'

Cam smiled, a big, happy smile. 'Who is?'

She could fall for that smile. So rare but when he tried it was beautiful. Which brought her to the next subject. 'I'm thinking I should be moving on soon. Saturday, maybe.' Huh? What had happened to going tomorrow? Saturday had slipped out so easily. She was finding it harder by the day to go. Cam had sucked her in, wrapped her in kindness, and made her start looking at the world differently. That was almost addictive.

Cam leant back in his chair and stared at her. 'Moving on? To where? Not to mention how. You can't drive yet.'

'I don't want to overstay my welcome.' *Lame, Jenny, very lame.*

'I'll let you know when you have.' That smile had well and truly disappeared now, making her sad.

'Now, why doesn't that surprise me?' She tried for a light-hearted tone. Big fail. 'Seriously, Cam, you've done more than enough for me. Think about what you said regarding the twins and them connecting with me. Wouldn't it be better for me to go now, before it becomes a problem?'

Where had that come from? She hadn't consciously thought it through, but now that the idea was out there she knew it to be true. 'No way do I want to upset Andrew and Marcus.'

'Low blow, Jenny Bostock.' He looked taken aback. Why? She was only trying to take his concerns into consideration.

'It wasn't meant to be.' *I don't want to go. Not yet.* But staying would only make her eventual leaving harder for her as much as for the boys. She just knew it. Already Cam featured in her daydreams, and her night-time ones. Even looking at him threw her sex-starved body into a pickle. Considering that sex had never been high on her list of requirements even in the good times, this was hard to understand. Could it be because she'd never met a man as hot as Cam? Just breathing the same air as him turned her on. *Hello? Who am I? I don't recognise myself.*

'What are you doing for Christmas?' Cam stretched his long legs further under the table and crossed his ankles.

'Christmas?' What did that have to do with anything?

'You know. The time when Santa Claus comes down the chimney, bringing sacks of presents for everyone.'

She nodded. 'That Christmas.' Maybe she should go tonight. Christmas used to be filled with fun and love. She couldn't imagine sitting down to unwrap those presents or to eat roast turkey and hot ham without Alison. Last year the whole issue had been avoided when Mum and Dad had joined her and Colby at a restaurant on Auckland's viaduct.

'It's not far off. Have you got plans?'

Stop right there, Cameron.

'Yes, I have, as it happens.'

I'm going to book into a hotel in some place I've never visited before and spend the day exploring.

Disappointment gleamed out at her from those all-seeing eyes. An uncomfortable silence settled between them, making her fidgety. Finally, when she couldn't bear it any more, she said, 'What are you and the boys doing that day?' Turn it on him, divert his attention.

'Going down the Kenepuru Sound to the family beach house with the whole Roberts clan.'

'You've got brothers and sisters?'

'Three sisters, three brothers-in-law, six nieces

and nephews, and my parents. We have a wonderful time.'

She'd got an answer that only caused envy to unfurl deep inside her. Family. Mum and Dad. Back in Dunedin. Christmas would be as lonely for them there as it would be for her in a hotel. She made an instant decision. 'I'm going down south to see my parents.'

'Good idea.' But she noted a hint of disappointment in Cam's eyes before he turned back to the computer and began tapping on the keyboard.

Dismissed. Fair enough. She hadn't exactly been forthcoming about her off-the-cuff plans. Taking the blunt hint, she hobbled towards the hallway. 'Goodnight.'

'Jenny,' Cam called softly. 'Don't make any definite plan about when you're leaving. Stay for the weekend and see how you feel next week. The boys would love to have you here for their school swimming competition on Saturday.'

Yeah. But what about Cam? Would he love to have her standing with him as he encouraged his lads to swim faster?

CHAPTER EIGHT

CAM FELT FREER than he had for months. His boys were happier than they'd been since arriving in Havelock and that was saying something because they enjoyed living in this tiny place where everyone knew everyone—sometimes far too well. The kids were the only reason he'd hung in here, putting them before the aching need to lose himself in a city filled with people and action and work. Yet today there was a lightness in his chest around his heart that had nothing to with Havelock and a lot to do with the woman walking beside him.

'Hi, Cam,' Braden greeted him, as he placed his 'OPEN' sign outside his tourist info centre. 'You're looking pleased with yourself this morning.'

'Christmas is just around the corner, the sun's shining and my boys are in the swimming team for this weekend's contest against Rai Valley School. Can't get better than that.'

'Sounds like you're taking happy pills,' Jenny muttered.

He laughed. Out loud. A deep belly laugh. What the heck? Maybe he had swallowed something he shouldn't have. Braden probably wore a shocked look on his face after that spewing of words he'd given. He shrugged. Tough. 'I'd better get that bottle of multivitamins checked out. Who knows what's in them?'

'Maybe you need to see a doctor.' Jenny shook her head at him. 'I know of one who thinks you're decidedly off your rocker. Braden's still scratching his head and staring at you as though he doesn't know you any more.'

'Does that doctor accept responsibility for my deterioration?'

Those gorgeous green eyes widened, and laughter crinkles appeared at their corners. 'You're blaming me for your suddenly apparent motor-mouth?'

'Of course I am.' Not only that. He blamed her for the hours he lay awake at night, wishing she was lying naked in his bed with her legs entwined with his and his hands on those beautiful mounds pushing out the front of her skimpy top.

'Great.'

'Boys, watch where you're going,' he said automatically, before taking Jenny's elbow to lead her across the road after a truck and trailer unit loaded with pine logs rolled past.

Not that she needed his helping hand, despite having left the crutches at home this morning, but he liked doing it, enjoyed touching her. Her skin was smooth and soft under his fingers. The pulse at her elbow rapped a beat on his fingertip and heated his blood fast. Resisting the urge to drop her elbow or the other one to hold on tighter, he just enjoyed the moment, and ignored the sudden intake of breath she made.

The other side of the road came all too quickly, giving him no excuse to continue holding her. But Jenny was ahead of him, tugging free before he had time to loosen his fingers. She stepped sideways, putting a gap between them. Not happy with him? He tried to read her expression, found he couldn't. She didn't appear to be angry. Good, because he really didn't want them getting offside. 'What are you going to do today?'

She flicked him a wry smile. 'I'll have a nana nap, wash my bloomers and scrub my dentures.'

No mention of attempting to cook dinner again. Phew. 'That exciting, huh?' If she was joking with him he had to be in her good books. So taking her elbow hadn't been a bad thing. Did that mean he'd sparked some heat in her as she had done in him? *I hope so. Oh, boy, as I've told myself before, I'm in trouble.* 'Don't nana nap through three o'clock and miss meeting the boys at school.'

'Maybe I'll wait outside the gate all day so I'll be sure to be there on time. Where do they get all that energy?'

The boys had raced ahead, joining other kids on their way to school. 'No idea, but I could do with some of it.' Yet today there was a spring in his step as he tracked the daily route to the medical centre. Until now Havelock had been little more than an anchor around his neck. Today he found himself looking around, smiling at people, watching Jenny as she hobbled along the uneven path, enjoying the twins' enthusiasm for school. Today he actually liked Havelock: liked that he lived here, was making a life for himself and the kids here. Liked walking to work with this woman.

A family. That's what this felt like. Family. How he'd always hoped it would be with Margaret. He shivered, looked up to see if the sun had gone behind a cloud. Nope, not a cloud anywhere to be seen. The ghost had been his dreams and aspirations. Margaret had doused all of those.

Yet here he'd been feeling warm and fuzzy about a family when the woman who'd triggered this was all but a stranger to him. More than crazy, considering his ex hated this ridiculously small place that she believed no one had heard of. No one that counted anyway. Jenny was used to big hospitals and people in her face all the time so it was given that she was unlikely to feel comfortable in Havelock. He needed to remember that next time his hormones woke up.

'See ya, Dad.' Andrew flapped a hand in his direction.

Blink. Oh, right. His corner. 'Wait,' he called to the boys. 'The medical centre's up this street,' he told Jenny. 'I appreciate you doing this. It's one of the things that I worry about: Andrew and Marcus having to go to Amanda's and not being able to come straight home from school. But there's no other way around the problem.'

'The pleasure's all mine.' She sounded so sincere his heart melted a weeny bit more.

Note to self: don't feel bad when Jenny finally leaves. Enjoy the time she's here with us.

Jenny clomped along to the school gate a few minutes before three. It was Thursday and she wasn't at all ready to leave. In fact, she was getting far too comfortable in the Roberts household. It felt like home. Maybe come Monday she'd feel differently. The weekend was bound to be hectic and crazy.

Standing close to but not in the midst of the parents waiting for their children, she glanced around and chuckled. This whole pick-up-the-kids-from-school scene had absolutely nothing to do with her previous life. But when the boys had asked if she would and Cam had agreed if Jenny was happy with the idea, she hadn't been able to come up with any reason why not.

'Hi, I'm Amanda. The twins usually come to me after school. I'm presuming you're Jenny, right?' A woman with bright orange stripes in her black hair stood in front of her.

'Hello, Amanda. Guess the cast's a giveaway, huh?'

Amanda grinned. 'The twins talk nonstop about you. I reckon there's not much about you I don't know.'

Absolutely wonderful. So all the town knew she'd lost her mojo and her sister. 'How boring for you all.'

The grin widened, if that was possible. 'Relax. The twins think you're pretty, and cool for reading to them, and apparently you're hopeless at cooking. Sometimes I wish I couldn't put a meal together then someone else would have to feed my tribe.'

'There is that. But you wouldn't believe the mess I made of dinner and the kitchen the other night. No wonder the boys were talking about me.'

'I heard dinner went in the bin untouched.'

So it was true what people said—there were no secrets in small towns. A piercing ringing sound came from inside the school grounds. Saved by the bell. Now all she had to do was wait for Marcus and Andrew to find her and then they could go home—where she could make some more blunders to amuse everyone.

Amanda said, 'Why don't you come and have a coffee with me tomorrow morning? I do a mean cappuccino, even if I say so myself.'

About to say no, Jenny glanced at this woman who had been kind enough to speak to her. There was nothing but friendship in her eyes. 'I'd like that.'

Yeah, actually, she would. It had been a long time since she'd met a friend for coffee, and while she and Amanda weren't strictly friends it would be nice all the same. Another tick for Havelock. This small place had started doing what nowhere else had managed so far. It had begun chipping away her armour plating that kept the world out and her pain in.

As Amanda gave her the address children swarmed out the gate to surround the waiting parents, the noise level getting higher by the second.

'Jenny, we're hungry.'

At least that's what she thought Marcus said, but who'd know in the bedlam? He could've told her he'd lost his school bag or his lunch had been stolen, she wouldn't have a clue. 'Just as well I brought my wallet, then, isn't it? We can stop at the bakery on the way home.'

'Can we really?' Andrew bounced up in front of her.

'Better than me making you some biscuits.' She grinned.

Andrew nodded solemnly. 'Would they look like that chicken thing you threw out?'

'Probably.' What happened to the Jenny who hated to fail at anything? The Jenny who didn't do cooking so that no one could laugh at her messes? She'd come to Havelock, that's what.

The boys talked nonstop until they reached the bakery, where they had an endless debate about which treat they'd like. Finally Jenny chose a custard square for herself, saying, 'You've got until the lady gives me my cake to make up your minds, otherwise you're going without.'

Funny how quickly they decided on the brownie. 'Thanks, Jenny.'

'What's for dinner?' Andrew asked, less than a minute later.

'We'll have to wait and see,' she told them. 'You haven't eaten your brownie yet.'

Marcus rolled his eyes at his brother. 'It's Thursday. Sausage night.'

What? 'You have the same thing on the same night? All the time?'

'Of course.'

Probably the only way Cam coped. He was a thoroughly organised man about the house. Already she'd come to recognise his routines for getting the dinner on, the house tidied, the boys showered and their homework under way.

'Hope you don't mind the meals we have here,' Cam said later that night, as he pulled a packet of mince from the freezer.

'Meat patties tomorrow night, then?'

'You've worked it out already?' Cam's smile was wary. 'I do vary the menu occasionally. It's also different from summer to winter. I make mostly casseroles in the colder months, which are great for being able to slow-cook in the crockpot all day.'

'You're very well organised.' Her routine used to involve going to the supermarket every day after work, where there were all manner and number of solutions for meals and drinks.

'You avoided my original question.'

Handing Cam his mug of tea, she laughed. 'Relax. I'm hardly going to complain, am I? You might tell me to get my own dinner and that would be a disaster.'

'You've *never* cooked?' He did look a little bamboozled by the thought of that.

'You're asking because I'm female and all good women are goddesses in the kitchen?' Her hair swirled around her face as she shook her head. 'Not me. Why bother learning when supermarkets shelves are filled with so many options for heat-and-eat meals? They mightn't be gourmet but compared to what I create they're delicious.'

Heat slipped up his neck and into his cheeks. 'I didn't mean to be all gung-ho over whose role is whose in the house. I enjoy cooking, especially when I'm not rushing around like a lunatic, trying to get everything done so I can get to bed before midnight.' He shrugged. 'There's something special about putting together a meal to share with family or friends. For me it's a way of showing I care.' Another shrug. 'Even if I only barbecue some sausages.'

She hadn't thought of it that way. Sharing with family or friends. She used to share flowers from her garden. That had always made her feel good and hopefully it had done the same for the people she'd given them to. 'I can see how that might be. Except I'd probably lose any friends I might have. Can you imagine sitting down to eat that chicken chasseur I somehow managed to destroy?'

His nose wrinkled and his mouth curved ever so slightly upwards. 'Truthfully? No. It had a distinctly unappealing look to it. Cooking rule number one: remember that people eat with their eyes before they pick up their knife and fork.'

Rule one, eh? 'So it's all about presentation.'

'Yep. You can fool people quite a lot if the plate looks appetising.'

The next morning Jenny swung into Amanda's large kitchen and stopped to gape at the array of cookery books on the shelves. 'You must have hundreds of books.'

'I should really go through them and toss the

older ones out but I can't bring myself to do it.' Amanda jammed her hands on her hips as she joined Jenny in staring at the collection. 'So many recipes and no time to read them, let alone use them.'

'Does everyone in Havelock like cooking?' The bakery was beyond excellent; Cam wasn't adverse to putting a meal together; and now this. From a wooden rail above the central island gleaming pots and pans hung off hooks within easy reach of anyone working at the bench. 'Unbelievable.'

'I used to be a chef before I had four kids and took on teaching swimming.' Behind the orange and black hair was obviously a very smart brain.

'You wouldn't go back into a kitchen here in Havelock?'

As the nostril-twitching aroma of good coffee filled the kitchen, Amanda crossed to a cupboard and found some cups. 'No. It would take most of my time and I far prefer being here for the children. They're growing up so fast already that they'll be gone out into the big, wide world before I know it, and to have wasted these years in a commercial kitchen would be gutting.'

There was a truth in that. Amanda's focus was family, whereas she didn't have to think about anyone else. Yet in the past week she'd started to reach out to Mum and Dad with daily emails that were long, wordy ramblings about her stay with the Roberts family. A family that she was trying to help in any little way she could, even if Cam ran such an organised household that there was little she actually did that made any difference.

'Amanda...' Jenny paused. Was she about to ask something impossible? Not to mention stupid? 'Would you show me how to cook a couple of simple meals that I could prepare for Cam and the boys? I'll pay for everything. If you have the time, of course.'

The woman didn't even hesitate. Not so bright in that orange head after all? 'That would be fun. When do you want to start?'

Oh. Um. Next week? But what if she'd gone by then? 'Today?'

Again, no hesitation. 'Drink your coffee and we'll discuss what we're having for dinner to-night.'

'We will?' Eek. What had she done? Her?

Cooking? Yeah, why not? 'I'm absolutely hopeless in a kitchen. Like, really and truly useless.' She'd make a total stuff-up and Amanda would regret agreeing to show her the basics. *Shush, Amanda's talking.*

'I've an idea. I make meals that suit the kids as well as Ross and myself. Why don't we make twice as much and you take home enough for Cam and his lads? That way I can talk you through the process and I'm not having to think up two different meals every time.'

'Sounds perfect.' Every time? Would there be more than one chance at this? Warmth flooded her. Was she really about to embark on a cooking lesson? Unbelievable. 'This coffee's great.'

'Told you it would be.' Amanda grinned. 'Do you like beef stroganoff?'

'I love it. Would Marcus and Andrew like that?'

'My kids can never get enough of it so I'm sure the twins will be the same. They might've had it here some time.'

Uh-oh. 'I'll have to cook rice.'

'Get a rice cooker. I've got one somewhere I'll lend you for starters.'

* * *

The rice was white and fluffy. The beef melted in her mouth. And Cam and the boys had seconds. Jenny couldn't stop smiling.

'That was yummy. So you bought a packet with instructions in English.' Cam gave her the biggest smile yet. One that went all the way down to the tips of her toes.

Shaking her head at him, she gave a return smile. 'No packets involved. That was the real article. Made from scratch.'

His eyebrows rose distressingly high. His eyeballs might pop out if he wasn't careful. 'Have you been pulling my leg about your cooking skills?'

'Nope. This morning I had a lesson from an ex chef.' Wow, she felt good. Not only had she done something other than wipe down benches for this wonderful man but she'd knocked back one of her gremlins. She could cook—with a lot of help from Amanda. *Easy, girl: pride before a fall. One dinner does not make a competent cook.*

'You've been talking to Amanda.' Cam's eyebrows returned to their natural position.

'More like listening as she explained how to slice beef across the grain, and not to over-stir the sauce ingredients. I've had a great day.' A really great day. 'Oh, except Amanda managed to slice three fingers while showing me how fast she was at chopping onions.'

'I take it you weren't required to sew her digits back on?' Cam's eyebrows rose and his mouth curved into a heart-warming smile.

'She refused to even consider stitches so I made some butterfly plasters from her first-aid kit supplies.' It hadn't been a major incident but she'd felt good to have been able to help Amanda medically. The doctor part of her make-up seemed to be waking up here in Havelock too. 'Amanda won't be using her left hand for much over the next few days.'

'Knowing that woman, I wouldn't bet on it. I'm glad you were there for her.'

'Me, too.' Yeah, and leaving Cam just got a whole lot harder. Seeing those smiles as they'd all tucked into dinner had warmed her deep inside in a way she'd never felt, even before Alison's death. This warmth came with a sense of belonging. Finding her mojo?

Maybe I won't leave. Oh, sure, I'm going to settle down in Havelock, lift the population number to five hundred and one, and do what exactly? Sell beef stroganoff at the gate? Like a pricked balloon her happiness shrivelled in on itself. She had to leave soon.

Cam gathered up the plates and stood up. 'That was the tastiest meal we've had in this house. Go, you.' In the kitchen he sluiced the dishes and said quietly, 'The boys love having you bring them home after school, by the way. I prefer it for them. Adds to the stability of their lives, which has been a roller-coaster ride so far.'

Stunned at him even admitting that, she held her breath while thinking about what he'd revealed. She'd wanted to help Cam out, but in this way? The connotations were huge. Doing this involved trust and care and could wreck those little boys' hearts again when she was gone.

'Maybe I shouldn't do it any more. Have you thought how they'll feel when I go away?' *She* was going to feel awful. Leaving the boys would be hard. Leaving Cam—well, she couldn't begin to imagine how that would feel. She suspected gut-wrenching wouldn't begin to describe it.

'I have, but I'm banking on the summer holidays being long enough they won't be at all perturbed.'

Right, he had it all sorted. Except, 'I won't be here until the end of term.'

'You sound very sure.'

'I am.' And because she owed him, she added, 'There's some place I absolutely have to be. No argument.'

'I see.' It was evident in his eyes that he didn't see at all. How could he? He knew nothing about what drove her.

'I'll clean up the kitchen if you've got other things to get done.' She stood up and rubbed the small of her back where it had been aching for a while.

Cam's gaze followed her hands as she rubbed up and down, working her fingers into the tight muscles. He swallowed hard and pressed his lips tight. The plates in his hands banged onto the bench. She bit down on the reluctant smile about to break across her mouth. It wouldn't do for him to know she'd noticed his reaction. They couldn't follow through. Because of the children. Because she wasn't ready. Because she was leaving and flings, even very short ones, weren't on her agenda. But that didn't mean she couldn't find some sweet pleasure in having him a little bit attracted to her.

He made her feel alive again, reminded her she was a woman, not just someone traipsing the country looking for forgiveness and the incentive to return to medicine.

The only person who has to forgive you is you.

The salt and pepper shakers dropped from her hand onto the table with a bang. What? Where had that dumb idea come from? Not her, that's for certain. Mum and Dad must hold her responsible for Alison's death. Didn't they? They'd never come out and said so but she'd been the only person there when it had happened so, of course, she should've been able to do something to save Alison.

'Jenny? What is it?' Cam was at her side, pushing her gently back onto the chair she'd just risen from. 'What's going on?'

She snapped her mouth shut before she could spill the words that would tell him what a dreadful sister she'd been, not to mention a useless doctor. That would certainly remove any hint of attraction he might feel for her, and she really didn't want to lose that. Not yet. In a few days' time when she went away she'd deal with that. But not tonight. Not now. 'I'm fine. Just moved too fast and cricked my ankle.'

Cam made his usual move and pressed a finger under her chin, raising her face so he could lock eyes with her. 'Try again. I don't believe it.' There was nothing but concern and compassion looking out at her, but she wouldn't fall for it. She had to be strong. Despite telling him about the accident that had taken Alison, she'd not filled him in on all the gruesome details and she wasn't about to start. They were her horrors to deal with, no one else's. Especially not this man's, who'd done nothing but show her kindness.

Pushing his hand aside, she stood again. 'Then we'll have to agree to disagree.' Snatching up the salt and pepper, she slipped past him into the kitchen and started rinsing off dishes. *Please go and find another chore to do, preferably one in another room. Leave me to myself for a bit. I'll come right quicker that way.*

But when she turned around Cam stood right

there in front of her, that concerned expression on his face changing, morphing into…? 'What?'

'Jenny.' His hands touched her cheeks, oh, so lightly. 'You're beautiful,' he whispered, as he moved his head closer.

This wasn't what she'd meant when she'd wanted him to find another chore. This was… She leaned closer. This was… The air seemed to vibrate between them. Those brown eyes were locked on hers, watching, waiting, wanting. This was—*is*—right.

Her mouth brushed those lips she'd been dreaming for days of kissing. Brushing her mouth over Cam's wasn't enough. Hunger gripped her. Thankfully Cam began kissing her properly, hard and soft, demanding and giving. Knee-buckling sensations tore through her like wildfire. Heat rose to warm her face. Wrapping her arms around him, she held on for dear life, kissing him back as hard and soft, as demanding and giving as he kissed her. His mouth was hot, hot, hot. His hands on her waist were hot. His chest pressing against her breasts was hard and hot.

And lower down something else seemed to be

heating up too, definitely hardening if that bulge pushing into her stomach was anything to go by. How did two mouths touching cause wild reactions south of their waists? Because right in her centre that heat had turned molten, setting her muscles to squeezing and her hormones dancing.

'Yuck, they're kissing.'

'Don't look. That's gross.'

Cam set her back from him so fast it took a moment to regain her equilibrium. Marcus and Andrew. Oh, hell. Now they'd blown it. What were the boys going to think about this? A quick look at Cam told her he already regretted coming near her. The heat suffusing her body rapidly chilled down to cool. Great. She'd definitely be packing her bag now. Hopefully Cam would wait until the morning before kicking her out on the street.

'Marcus, Andrew, where's your homework?' Cam sounded like he was in control of his emotions.

Too in control. Like that kiss hadn't affected him one little bit. But he had been reacting to her as though he wanted her. Or had it been that

long for him as it had for her that his body had
just woken up all by itself?

'Do we have to do it?'

'There's that swimming competition tomorrow.'

'Go and get it. Now,' Cam snapped.

Jenny snatched up the dishcloth and began
wiping down the bench. The sooner the kitchen
was cleaned up the sooner she could escape to
her room and close the door on this monumental error she and Cam had made. Yes, Cam had
a lot to answer for. She hadn't started the kiss,
couldn't take all the responsibility for their
actions. But one quick peek at his face and she
knew she'd better make herself scarce. For now
at least.

Cameron watched Jenny from where he supervised the boys' homework. Her shoulders were
tense as she swiped at the bench with the cloth.
But just when he thought she was going to spit
the dummy out a tiny smile widened that delicious mouth and lifted the corners. So she had
enjoyed their stolen kiss. Damn the boys for their
interruption. Then again, thank goodness they

had burst into the room, otherwise who knew where kissing Jenny might've led? Apart from down the hall to his bedroom, that was. Except those boys were the very reason why it had had to stop when it had. Damn it again.

Note to self: find a time and place where there are no boys so he could repeat that kiss with the hottest woman he'd had the pleasure of knowing.

Note to self: do it soon.

CHAPTER NINE

THE SWIMMING RACES were hilarious to watch. Boys and girls everywhere looked excited and terrified and determined to do well in their events.

Jenny waved. 'Good luck, Marcus. Good luck, Andrew.'

They waved back. Cam gave them the thumbs-up. 'Give it your best shot, guys.' Then, in an aside, he said, 'If only they weren't in the same race. They'll be arguing about the result for days. Marcus swims like a fish while Andrew's more like a concrete block.'

'You haven't tried asking the teacher to separate them?' Hard to believe none of last night's tension had carried over into today. They'd both got up in a great frame of mind, preparing the boys for the swimming and strolling down the main road to the school as though they did it every day.

'On many occasions. Apparently I don't know what I'm talking about.'

Jenny nudged him with an elbow. 'Look at them poised ready to leap in. Like pros they are.' If only she and Cam did do this every day. Not the swimming but taking the boys to school and sharing whatever they were into.

'They watch too much sport on TV, that's what.' Cam's gaze was fixed on his boys.

Say what he liked, Jenny felt sure that was pride swelling his chest. A muscular chest that she'd love nothing more than to run her fingers all over, and tease those nipples till he groaned with need. She definitely had to catch the eleven o'clock bus to Blenheim on Monday. Or should she go back to Nelson and wait out the days till it was time to visit Kahurangi?

'On your marks.' A whistle sounded. The kids were off, some leaping into the water, others belly-flopping, and then there was Marcus. He dived, not neatly but it was a dive.

Jenny grinned. 'Go, Marcus. You're one cool kid.' Hell, *her* chest was swelling with something like pride. 'Where's Andrew?' It was hard to see him amongst the splashes and mini-waves made by the various swimming styles.

'Five metres down his lane. The one with the arms like a windmill having hiccups.'

Andrew might have the most ungainly technique and his legs might be closer to the bottom of the pool than the surface of the water but he was making progress. 'Go, Andrew. Come on, you can do it.' Jenny leapt up and down on her good foot, her hands above her head, waving at him. 'You, too, Marcus. What a champ. You're winning.' Of course, neither of them could see or hear her but she didn't care. This was exciting.

Cam roared his encouragement. 'Come on, Marcus. Ten metres to go. That's it. You're a champ.' Then his gaze cruised down the pool to latch onto Andrew. 'Keep going, my boy. One arm after the other.'

Jenny reached for Cam's hand. 'We should be at the finish line—or whatever you call it in swimming. Those boys are going to want to see you standing there, smiling at them.'

Cam's fingers instantly interlaced with hers. 'You're right.'

They got to the end of the pool as Marcus

hauled himself out of the water. 'Did you see that, Dad? I won.'

Cam ruffled Marcus's hair. 'Well done, kiddo. That was a great race.'

Marcus beamed at him then turned to her. 'Did you see me, Jenny?'

'I saw you. You're like a seal in the water.' Jenny dropped a kiss on his forehead, got a whiff of chlorine and immediately recalled the many hours she and Alison and their mates had spent at the local pool in the summer holidays.

A warm hand covered her shoulder, warm fingers on her skin. Cam bent his head so his mouth was close to her ear. 'You're a marvel with these two. Sure you haven't got a gang of kids hidden somewhere?'

She heard the words but couldn't answer for the effect his warm breath was having on her skin. Inside, a gentle wave of warmth quickly became a tsunami of heat, rolling through her, overwhelming her ability to stand upright. Just like last night, only this time it hadn't even taken Cam's kiss to start her off. Placing a hand on Cam's arm for balance, she struggled to gain control. When her eyes locked with his she hoped she didn't look as startled as he did right now. How could one touch, one look make her feel so—so stunned?

'Dad?'

The twins. She gasped at the same instant Cam swung his head up. Her heart pounded. What had just gone down? Here, at the pool. Totally out of place. They were at the school, surrounded by kids and teachers and parents. And Marcus and Andrew. Far worse than in the kitchen last night.

Cam calmly dropped his hands to his sides. 'I'd better get a move on.' He had to be in Blenheim for the afternoon clinic. 'See you tonight, okay?'

'Is Jenny staying to watch us some more?'

'I'll be here for the rest of the afternoon.'

'Cool. We're going to have a bombing contest after the last race.'

She heard Cam say, 'Be careful,' in a worried tone.

'I'll make sure they behave.' She looked directly at him. 'No broken bones on my watch.'

His smile was strangely relaxed, like he didn't care if half of Havelock had witnessed that near kiss. It seemed for ever before he looked away and focused on the boys. 'How about I get fish and chips on the way home and we can take Jenny down to the marina to eat them?'

The shouts of *yes* were deafening. The warmth returned to her body, this time calm and gentle. This family seemed to like having her around. What's more, she loved being here, with them. Especially with the man who had woken up parts of her body she'd hardly been aware existed before. How could desire for one man be so different from any other she'd experienced in her previous sexual encounters?

'I hear you made a fabulous dinner last night.' Amanda appeared before her moments after Cam disappeared around the corner of the school building, looking too smug for her own good.

Glad of the distraction, Jenny agreed. 'It was delicious, and everyone except me ate two helpings. Thank you so much. You have no idea how much I appreciate it.'

'It seems to have had a strange effect on you and Cam, if what I overheard the twins telling their mates is true.' Amanda's eyes glittered with amusement.

'Here I'd been hoping we'd get away with that little adventure.'

Amanda laughed. 'Not a chance. I doubt there's a living soul in town who doesn't know you two were kissing last night.'

Shrugging, Jenny joined in the laughter. 'Guess there's nothing I can do about it. I'm not going to wish it hadn't happened.' Oh, where'd her discretion button gone? It wasn't as though she usually went around telling others about her private life. 'How are those fingers?'

'Very sore, but they get me out of washing dishes.'

'Wonder what we can cook next.'

'How about lasagne on Monday?' Amanda asked.

'That's getting more difficult, isn't it?' *Walk before running, remember?*

'Not at all. You'll be fine with it. Come and meet some of the other mums. Be warned, they're curious about you, especially after the stories and that eye-locking moment you just had with Cam.'

Jenny groaned. 'Great. Think I'd better be making tracks for home.' *It is not home. And you told the boys you'd be watching them, re-member?* Oh, hell. She'd just agreed to go to Amanda's on Monday when she intended leaving that day. She guessed the buses ran the same on Tuesdays.

'We're keeping an eye on our kids from the other side of the pool under the shade sail.'

'Are they going to tease me, too?'

'You can bet your dinner on it.' Amanda grinned. 'Might as well face the firing line and get it done with.'

It should've felt exactly like that but the women were so friendly Jenny relaxed immediately when Amanda introduced everyone.

'Shelley, Karen, Jocelyn, meet Jenny. She's staying with Cam and the boys until her foot's come right.'

Fobbing off the comments about hot doctors, Jenny found a spot on the grass beside Shelley and carefully lowered herself to the ground.

'How's that ankle coming along?' Shelley asked.

'Not nearly fast enough.' Though if it had healed in three days, like she'd wanted, then she'd be long gone and back out on the road heading for the next town. And not getting to know Cam as much as she had.

Then Shelley asked her, 'Have you got kids? You seem to know what you're doing with Cam's two.'

'None yet.' Yet? 'Got to find a man first.' Why did Cam come to mind so instantly? *Don't answer that.* She couldn't anyway, not having a clue. An image of strong leg muscles and a tight butt burst across her brain. Okay, maybe a little clue.

'Looks to me like you already have.' Jocelyn had a nice smile even when being cheeky.

Amanda had no problem with giving an opinion on Jenny's single status either. 'Cam doesn't have anyone in his sights. You could check him out more thoroughly.'

Been there, done that, and so far liked what she'd seen, tasted, felt. 'I think the man's too busy to find time for dating. Anyway, I'll be gone within a few days.' How many times had she said that in the past week? The day that she packed her bag never seemed to come, always getting pushed further out. But soon she would have to make arrangements for that rendezvous with her past.

Shelley looked surprised. 'You're not staying on once your ankle's better? I'm sure Cam could use your help at the practice.'

'I think Cam more than handles the centre. Besides, I was an emergency specialist, not a GP.' She shoved to her feet and looked around for the twins. Suddenly she'd had enough of idle chatter that seemed to focus on her too much. Next, these women would be wanting to know why she wasn't doctoring at the moment, and she wasn't ready to share that with them today. Or ever.

Shouts came from the pool. Children were staring into the water. Parents had leapt to their feet and raced closer. Jenny felt her heart thump against her ribs. Where were the boys? Her eyes searched the area as she made her way down to the edge of the pool, found Andrew. Marcus? There, by the changing shed. Phew.

'Lily,' Shelley screamed, and pushed past Jenny to kneel down on the edge of the pool.

A man leapt into the pool, dived deep, aiming for the child on the bottom. The water was turning red down there.

'What happened?' Jenny asked the woman beside her. 'I'm a doctor, I can help.'

'I know. I think Lily was running along the edge and slipped. How many times do we have to tell the kids running is banned around the pool?'

'Can you call the ambulance? I'll do what I can but Lily is going to need oxygen and things that I don't have with me.' If she hasn't drowned down there.

'On it.' The woman was already punching 111 on her cell. 'The ambulance is just next door but the call will go through Christchurch.'

'I suppose it would be asking too much for someone here to have a key?' Jenny asked.

'I've got one. I'm Brett, a volunteer crew member. Simone, tell the dispatcher you've got the ambulance sorted but they still need to record the call.' The man turned to Jenny. 'What do you need?'

'A backboard, oxygen, neck brace, and the defibrillator just in case.'

Brett grabbed a woman by the arm. 'Give us a hand.'

Jenny squatted awkwardly beside Shelley. 'Your daughter?'

'Yes. Is she going to be all right?'

That was the million-dollar question. 'She hasn't been down there more than a few seconds.' But what was causing the bleeding?

Lily was quickly brought to the surface. Thankfully her rescuer had lifted her with his hands under her arms and saved her spine from curving. Now to keep her that way. 'Someone take her for me,' the man called.

'Give her to me.' Shelley reached for her daughter.

'Mummy!' Lily screamed.

'Wait.' Jenny grabbed Shelley's shoulder. Thank goodness Lily was breathing. One less problem. 'Sorry, Shelley, but we have to do this properly in case there's any spinal damage.' Looking around, she said, 'Once we get the backboard I need three people in there to place it against Lily and lift her out.'

Instantly hands were raised, and people were saying, 'I'll help.'

She pointed to the nearest three. 'Get into the water away from Lily so you don't cause her needless movement. Then I want you to stand behind her with…?'

'John.'

'With John. I'll come in and put a neck brace on her before you move her.' She bent down to remove her shoe.

Someone tapped her on her shoulder. 'Here you go. One neck brace. The backboard and everything you asked for. I'll go in with the neck brace. You keep that cast dry.' Brett gave her no time to reply, already sliding into the pool and pushing towards Lily.

Once Jenny saw Brett knew what he was doing she turned to get the backboard. Passing it down when he nodded, she held her breath as the girl was gently moved upwards and out to the side of the pool.

Shelley grabbed her hand and held on tight. 'She's bleeding from the head. That's serious, isn't it?'

Jenny squeezed back and looked around for Amanda. 'Can you take care of Shelley?' she mouthed.

Amanda joined them immediately, wrapping an arm around Shelley. 'Hang in there, and try not to panic. I'm sure Jenny knows what she's doing.'

'Can someone get a blanket out of the ambulance?' Jenny knelt beside the shivering, crying child. 'Lily, I'm Jenny and I'm a doctor. I want you to lie absolutely still for me. You mustn't move your head at all.' Even with the brace there was room for small movements.

'I want Mummy.' Lily coughed up water. 'Mummy,' she hiccupped.

Brett held her as still as possible but he couldn't prevent some movement. 'Careful, Lily.'

'Mummy's here, love.' Shelley's voice wavered as she crowded closer.

Jenny began gently feeling Lily's skull, looking for a soft patch where she might've hit the side of the pool. 'Tell me if it hurts when I'm touching you. Do you feel any pins and needles in your legs?'

'No. Why?'

'What about in your fingers?'

'No. Am I all right? Is that blood on my face?'

Lily's faced puckered up as tears spurted from her eyes. 'I don't like blood.'

'We'll clean it up for you in a minute, sweetheart.' The blood was pouring from a gash on Lily's forehead but at least the bone didn't appear to be broken. Still, only a scan would be able to totally eliminate that possibility.

'Want me to apply a pressure dressing to that wound?' Brett asked quietly. 'Meg can hold her head.'

She nodded. 'Yes. Are there any slings on board the ambulance?' She'd noticed Lily's elbow was twisted at a slightly odd angle.

'I'll get one.' Brett didn't waste time, just got on with what was needed.

She continued working her hands down the length of the girl's body but found no other injuries. 'Shelley, Lily will have to go to hospital. She needs stitches in her forehead and a cast on her arm. They'll take X-rays of that first and a scan of her head. But I'm tentatively optimistic she's one very lucky little girl.'

A flood of tears streamed down Shelley's face. 'Thank you, Jenny. I'm so glad you were here.'

Brett returned and she helped him tape the

pressure bandage on Lily's head, careful not to jar the child's neck. Then they carefully slipped the sling under her left arm and behind her neck. Not that Lily was about to leap up and run around but the sling would prevent unnecessary movement.

'There you go, Lily. Now, we're going to put you on a trolley and place you in the ambulance. Mummy will be with you all the time.' Twisting her head, she found Shelley standing almost on top of her. 'You okay with that?'

'Try and stop me.'

Amanda said, 'I'll take your other kids home with mine. What about Gavin? Want me to get hold of him to let him know what's going on?'

'Please. I think he's on the harvester, doing some maintenance to the line hauler. Tell him to come through to the hospital as soon as he can.'

Jenny placed her hands on her hips and leaned back, clicking her spine into place. Kneeling all that time hadn't been comfortable. Then she leant forward over Lily. 'I'll see you in a day or two, okay?'

She helped Brett and another guy carefully slide Lily onto the stretcher and watched as he wheeled her over to the ambulance, which was now parked at the entrance to the pool area.

'How do you stay so calm?' Amanda asked from beside her.

'Guess that comes with the training.' Though she had always been calm in emergency situations. If she was going to have a panic it would be after the event, not during it.

'Well, you mightn't be so flash at cooking but you sure know how to fix people.'

Yeah, she did, didn't she? Now that Lily was on her way to hospital and she could relax, she could feel a rush of excitement warming her. She'd helped Lily, made sure she was safe and comfortable. Had been ready if anything more serious occurred. Damn it, she felt good.

The boys ran up. 'Jenny, did you save Lily?'

'No, I just helped her.' She'd completely forgotten about the boys while all that had been going down.

'Relax. I had my eye on them,' Amanda told her.

'Them and half the school, it seems. But thanks. I'm easily distracted.'

'What's to eat?' Marcus asked. 'I'm hungry.'

'When aren't you?' She rubbed his mussed-up hair, which was so long it was in his eyes. 'You need a haircut.'

'Dad forgets to make us an appointment at Kaye's shop.'

'Is Kaye the hairdresser?' She'd noticed the small house on the main street that had been converted into a salon when she'd walked to the grocery store.

'It's a girls' place but lots of us go there,' Marcus told her.

'Where's Andrew?' Then she spied him chasing a ball around the field with three other boys. 'Shall we get him and head home with a stop at the bakery?'

'Andrew,' Marcus hollered. 'We're going to the bakery now.'

Guess that was a yes, then.

'Hey, who cut your hair?' Cam asked the moment he saw the twins. He'd never got around to making that appointment.

'Kaye. Jenny took us there after swimming.' Andrew screwed up his nose. He hated having his hair cut.

'I hope you behaved.'

'Yes, Dad. We did.'

'Where's Jenny?' The fish and chips needed to be eaten soon or they'd go soggy in their wrapping, and it would take ten minutes to walk down to the marina at her speed.

'I'm here,' her sweet voice called from the deck. 'Andrew, can you put the washing basket away, please?'

'Coming.' Andrew hopped off the couch and raced to do as Jenny asked.

Cam grinned at her. 'You'll have to tell me your secret. A haircut and putting the basket away without an argument. I don't believe it. Thanks a lot for the haircuts. I've been trying to remember to book them in for weeks.'

'Beginner's luck. Kaye had a cancellation.' She grinned back.

'Dad, Lily hit her head in the pool and Jenny saved her,' Marcus called from the kitchen.

Jenny winced. 'Lily slipped and went in, banging her head and elbow on the way.' She quickly filled him in on the details. 'I haven't rung the hospital yet to find out how the scan went.'

'I can do that, if you like. They're more likely

to tell me as I'm Lily's GP. But let's have dinner first.'

'Those fish and chips smell divine. I've put a few things together in your chilly bin. Drinks for the boys, wine for me and beer for you, a roll of paper towels for the messy faces, and some tomato sauce. Can you think of anything else?'

'Nothing at all. I'll grab the foldaway chairs and we'll be off.' A picnic. He was going on a picnic of sorts with his kids. And Jenny. His heart felt lighter than it had in yonks. This was fun, pure and simple. The kind of thing any dad should be doing with his boys, and yet he'd never thought to do it. By the time he got to the end of his working day he only wanted to get home and finish all the chores so he could relax for a bit. But with Jenny here he'd suggested it without considering the usual constraints he put on himself.

'Come on, slowcoach,' the woman slowly retraining him as a father called from the front door. 'I'm dribbling with anticipation of those chips.'

'Marcus, grab the box of tissues so we can wipe the slobber off Jenny's chin. We can't take her out in public looking like Socks when she's thrown up her biscuits.'

When Jenny picked up her crutches he frowned. He was being selfish, not considering she mightn't feel up to walking unaided. 'Want to take the car?'

'No way. I'm just being cautious after spending so long on my foot today. I'll toddle along behind you all so that by the time I get there you'll have my chair set up and my wine poured.' Then a furrow formed between her eyes. 'We are allowed to take our drinks onto the marina? I hadn't thought about that.'

'We'll be fine where we're going to sit.' The owner of the bar/café wouldn't mind them using his parking spot for their picnic. As that was attached to the licensed premises, they'd be legal.

'Good. I'll start hopping, then.'

Cam walked beside Jenny, happy to take as long as she needed to get where they were going, steamed fish and chips or not. 'You're going to have a few laughs at the marina. On Friday nights there's always a queue of people wanting to put their boats in the water so they can head out to their beach houses. Tempers get frayed and people try to queue jump. It can be entertaining, especially when someone mucks up backing their boat into the water.'

'Why is it that when you're backing a trailer or boat and people are watching you automatically make a botch-up of the job? I always do that.' Jenny's eyes were wide with anticipation. 'I'll enjoy watching others do the same thing.'

'That's not nice.' He laughed.

'Not at all.' Jenny grinned back at him, speeding up his heart rate. When she smiled or grinned those eyes became greener, warmer and sexier.

Now she asked, 'Do you own a boat?'

'One quarter of one. I've gone shares with my brothers-in-law. None of us uses it a lot, mostly to go to the family property for family holidays. It's a little bigger than what you'll see tonight so we've got a berth at one of the pontoons. We don't have to go through the hassle of lining up with everyone else. Or being laughed at by people like you.'

'Spoil my fun, why don't you?' Her thick hair swung around her face as she limped along. The long locks shone where the sun caught them, turning the shade almost fire-engine red, and tempting him to run his hand down them to see if his skin burned. Fortunately his brain put the brakes on that idea before he made an idiot of himself. Unfortunately it didn't stop him from wondering what it would be like to make love to her. His fascination had been growing daily to the point he needed to do something about it. Not actually touch her, but go for a hard run up the hill to the lookout. Get a sweat up doing something physical that didn't involve sex.

Who was he kidding? Since last night's kiss there wasn't a doubt in his mind that they should get up close and personal, and soon. It wasn't as though he was alone in his feelings. Jenny had responded to him as quickly as his own body had lit up.

Sex. Sex had been dominating every last one of his thought processes all day. But wanting to get up close and personal didn't make it a wise move. Jenny had never denied she'd be on her way soon. At least she'd been honest, which was what he wanted, right? Right. So should he make a play for Jenny? Or should he ignore his feelings?

Note to self: make up his mind.

CHAPTER TEN

'I CAN'T BELIEVE how long I've been in Havelock.' Astonishment made her laugh. Of all the places she'd visited she'd had to pick the tiniest to stop and smell the roses, or was that the salt air? But, of course, stopping hadn't been her doing. She couldn't deny she was enjoying being here, becoming involved in day-to-day routines with the Roberts family, and visiting Amanda most days. They were becoming firm friends. 'I might never want to leave.'

'Then don't,' Amanda said.

'It's not that easy.' *Why not? You have to stop some time, somewhere. You can go to Kahurangi and return here afterwards.* On the table her cell vibrated as she tried to squeeze the pasta dough through the rollers of the pasta machine. 'Bad timing.' She had flour from elbows to chin.

'Want me to grab it?' Amanda asked.

'Please.' The phone did ring occasionally these

days, usually the twins asking if she was meeting them after school, or had she looked in the laundry cupboard for her mojo yet?

'It's Cam. Something about an accident.'

Her heart dropped. Accident? Who was involved? Cam? The boys? She snatched the phone from Amanda. 'Cam? What's happened? Are you all right?'

Amanda shook her head at her. 'Of course he is. He's phoning you, isn't he?'

'Jenny, I'm fine. But one of the deckhands on Gavin Montrose's mussel harvester got caught in the ropes that haul up the mussel lines and could lose his arm. I'm heading out by boat immediately. I want you to come with me. This is emergency medicine—your kind of medicine—and the guy needs everything stacked on his side we can possible get.' Cam spoke urgently, as though his mind was already on the injuries he'd be seeing.

'I'm a little rusty.'

'Is there a reason you shouldn't do this?'

'No.' Nothing that sounded good enough for her not to help this guy. So stop vacillating. 'Pick me up at Amanda's gate.'

'I'm almost there.'

Closing the phone, she turned the tap on and started vigorously sluicing the flour off her arms. 'You heard?' she asked Amanda.

'Yep, and if you're not back by the time school's out I'll bring the boys here.'

Toot, toot.

'That'll be Cam. See you.'

'I hope you don't get seasick,' Cam said the moment she clambered into his vehicle. 'It's a bit rough out there.'

'Guess we're about to find out.' She snapped her seat belt in place. 'Why are we going by boat? Don't you have a rescue helicopter on call?'

'They'll have been called but we'll reach the harvester long before them. The helicopter has to come from Nelson or Wellington, about half an hour's flying time once they're off the ground.' Cam slammed on the brakes at the wharf. Out of the vehicle, he tossed the keys to a guy coming out of the harbourmaster's hut and grabbed a medical pack off the back seat. 'Park it for me, will you, George?'

They'd barely stepped on the boat and it was

pulling away from the jetty. 'This is going to be a very fast ride,' Cam shouted against her ear. 'Want to sit inside?'

'No.' She gripped the rail hard. 'I like to see where I'm going.'

Twenty minutes later they were in the Kenepuru Sound, slowing up to nudge beside a mussel harvester bobbing in the water beside lines held deep by laden mussel ropes. Hands reached down and hauled Jenny aboard with no finesse at all.

'On the other side,' the dishevelled-looking seaman grunted, and turned to pull Cam onto the deck.

Threading her way over and around any number of obstacles, breathing salty and fishy air, Jenny focused on what she was about see and the procedures she'd undertake. It all depended on the depth of damage the rope had done. 'What's the man's name?'

The seaman she was following tossed the name over his shoulder. 'Haydon Tozer.' Then the man stopped and turned back to them. 'The rope's still holding him down. We were afraid if we cut it then he'd bleed to death.'

'You've done the right thing.'

Haydon opened his eyes to a slit when Jenny reached him.

'Haydon, I'm Jenny, a doctor. This is Cameron, another doctor. We're going to get you out of here.' She lifted his good arm so she could take his pulse, all the time assessing the situation. The wire with all its weight had pulverised Haydon's forearm against a steel barrel.

Cam was already opening the medical pack and removing a mask as he asked, 'Can someone tell us what happened?'

Haydon answered. 'I was operating the winch when my sleeve got snagged and the next I knew I was caught like this.'

'Someone must've been quick to stop the wire.'

The man who'd hauled them aboard grunted, 'That'd be me.'

Haydon sat at an awkward angle so as to relieve as much tension on his shoulder and upper arm as possible. Jenny was surprised he was still relatively lucid.

'I'm going to give you some oxygen, mate.' Cam held up the mask.

'The arm's screwed, isn't it?' Haydon croaked

through his pain, and his eyes drifted shut. It was as though now help had arrived he was letting go the need to stay on top of everything.

Jenny winced internally. 'Let's check out the situation before I make comment.' But, yes, the sort of weight that rope carried suggested there was no alternative. She glanced at Cam. 'Pulse slow.' There was bound to be blood loss, even with pressure being applied by that rope.

Jenny pulled on gloves. 'I'm going to give you a nerve block so that you won't feel a thing while we get you sorted and out of here.' Which really said she'd already established she'd be amputating.

The guy's eyes opened for a brief moment then he nodded once.

Together she and Cam went through the ritual of checking off the drug dosage. As she plunged the needle into a muscle in Haydon's shoulder, Jenny was aware of the tension emanating off the crew, who stood to one side. She wondered how long they'd stay watching when she and Cam got the scalpels out. Hell, her stomach was rolling with nausea at the thought of removing

Haydon's arm, especially in a less than ideal situation.

'You're doing great,' Cam said quietly, as he handed her swabs to clean the skin at the site where she'd amputate.

Thank goodness for that. Cam's calmness steadied the last of her nerves. She briefly locked gazes with him and nodded.

'I'll hold him from behind.' One of the crew stepped forward.

'Great.' Cam tightened a ligature just above Haydon's elbow to slow to a minimum the blood loss that would occur as she operated. Drawing from his calmness, Jenny pressed the scalpel blade deep. As she worked to free their patient, Cam wiped up the blood that escaped the ligature's restraints.

It took for ever. Haydon slipped into semi-consciousness.

She'd never cut Haydon free. He'd die here. She worked harder.

At last. She stepped away so Cam could place a pad over the stump and tape that in place.

A loud thumping from above announced the

arrival of the rescue helicopter moments before the downdraught from the rotors lashed them.

'Doesn't the pilot know not to come so close?' she snapped, as she leaned over Haydon to protect him.

'I guess he doesn't have a lot of choice, given he's got to land the paramedic on this harvester,' Cam said a moment later, when the air settled again.

'How's our man doing?' she asked, feeling for a pulse.

'He's one toughie. Let's get him out of here.'

Then the paramedic was standing beside them, taking note of the details of the operation. 'We're taking him to Wellington. There's an orthopaedic surgeon already on standby.

There was a whirl of activity, getting Haydon belted onto a stretcher and raised to the helicopter. Jenny cleaned up the accident site and retrieved everything, placing it all in a bag to go to Wellington with Haydon. Then it seemed only minutes later she was climbing down into the boat and dropping onto a seat in the cabin. She slashed the back of her hand across her forehead. 'Phew. Glad that's over.'

Cam sat down beside her and reached for her hand. 'Me, too.' His thumb rubbed softly back and forth over her palm, like a windscreen wiper. 'Thanks for coming with me. I'd have hated being alone for that one.'

'Some things in medicine never get easy, do they?' She leaned her head against his shoulder. 'It's really only just begun for Haydon, though.'

'He's strong. Somehow I think he'll make the most of the situation and get on with living.'

'You make it sound easy.' Jenny stared at the floor. Was it that easy? Did picking up the pieces and getting on with her life all come down to attitude? 'Thanks for hauling my tail out here. It's been good for me. I felt like a doctor, thought like one, and acted competently.' That surprised her, and now she was very grateful for having had the opportunity. Could she be Dr Bostock again?

'You are a doctor. That was the neatest amputation I've witnessed, and given the circumstances you can be very proud.' Cam squeezed her hand and settled further down on the seat. 'I could do with a strong coffee about now.'

'Me, too.'

* * *

'You look pleased with yourself.' And absolutely gorgeous. Cam studied Jenny as he handed her a glass of wine. He looked forward to this half-hour with her at the end of each day when he could relax, talk medicine or boys or fishing. Not that she was into fishing, but she had let him ramble on about it last night until he'd caught her nearly falling asleep.

'Today, helping Haydon, it all came naturally, like I've never stopped practising. Following on from helping Lily the other day and, yeah, I do feel as though I'm getting my mojo back. Havelock's good for me.'

Cam thought so. Jenny looked more relaxed, less drawn than she had that day he'd brought her home with him. 'I enjoyed working with you.' He'd like the opportunity to do it again, though not if it meant someone had to lose an arm. He sipped his wine. 'I wonder how Haydon got on in surgery?'

'Can you find out?'

'I'll try, though not all medical personnel are forthcoming with details when they don't know me. So what did you do with the rest of the afternoon?'

'Had a coffee with Amanda and Shelley.'

'You're making friends with the whole village.' Maybe Jenny could settle here after all. She certainly didn't scoff at the people she met just because they were fishermen or factory hands. 'How was Shelley?'

'In a bit of a state about Haydon. No one seems to understand how it happened. They're so careful on that boat. She and Gavin have had a top rating for health and safety on their harvester and today's incident has gutted them. For Haydon as much as for them.' Her smile dimmed.

'There'll be an investigation by OSH.' Occupational Health and Safety would go over that harvester thoroughly.

'Shelley's flying across to Wellington in the morning to see Haydon and help with whatever he needs. I think they're going to suggest he comes back to stay with them when he's discharged,' Jenny added.

'That doesn't surprise me at all. It's how it is around here.'

She blinked at him. 'I have first-hand experience of that.' Her smile was cute and warming. 'I don't know how lucky I am sometimes.' Jenny twirled her glass between her fingers. 'I've been reminded of that today.'

Interested in getting to know more about what made her tick, Cam asked, 'Is this to do with why you are always restless? Why you're always talking about moving on when you don't need to?'

Her eyes darkened, her fingers whitened on the stem of her glass, and her lips mashed together as she stared out across the lawn.

Reaching for the glass, he removed it before the stem snapped and did some damage. 'Jenny?'

'I'll definitely be gone by the thirteenth.' Her voice was dead.

'Gone?' Within five days? Just when he'd begun to believe she might fit in here full time. What was going on? What had happened to her that was so bad she put up the shutters when he asked about her past? Did it have something to do with her twin? Draping an arm over her shoulders, he tucked her against him. 'Talk to me, Jenny. Tell me what happened. Tell me why you stopped being a doctor, why you're on the move.'

She pulled away, stood up. 'I'll get dinner ready. I'm sure the boys will be starving when they get home from Amanda's.'

'Wait. Talk to me,' he repeated. 'You've been with me for more than two weeks. We're becoming friends. I'd like to get to know you better. Is that such a bad thing?'

She stared down at him as though she'd never seen him before. 'I can't talk about it. Okay?'

Not at all. 'Can't or won't?'

'Does it matter? My sister died, my life stopped. That's all you need to know.'

'No, that answer's for others, not for me.' The hand he took in his was cold and shaky. All his doing, but he wanted to help her, to bring out that humour and fun that she occasionally let slip. Wanted to find the real Jenny Bostock. 'What's special about that particular date?'

She jerked her hand free, stepped further away from him. 'Which bit of leave it alone don't you get, Cam?' Her voice rose on his name. 'I am not prepared to talk about what happened. Ever. To anyone.'

That was so not healthy. But she wasn't about to have a heart-to-heart with him. That was so clear it glittered. Which hurt big time. What was apparent, though, was that this involved her sister. Anniversary of her death maybe? Fighting the urge to follow Jenny into the kitchen and keep trying to get her to talk, he sat staring out across the back yard and sipping his now tasteless wine.

Note to self: try to help Jenny through whatever has turned her life upside down.

He glanced inside, saw the saddest woman he'd ever encountered. The woman he suspected was coming to mean a lot to him. As in love? Did he love Jenny? Enough to get involved with whatever was tearing her apart?

Yes, he thought he did. Scrub that, he knew he did. Somehow, when he'd been trying so hard to keep her arm's length, she'd sneaked under the radar and stolen his heart.

To hell with it. Striding into the kitchen, he gently removed the stirring spoon from her hand and took her in his arms. 'I'm here for you, okay?' He didn't give her time to answer, just leaned down and captured her mouth with his.

Jenny stood absolutely still, not returning the kiss, but neither did she withdraw.

On her lips he tasted wine and Jenny, a heady mix that zoomed straight down his body, switching on his arousal. Somehow he didn't think this was the time for bedroom activities. His kiss had been about sealing his vow to look out for her, about showing he cared.

Her hands crept up his chest, smoothing over his muscles till she touched his neck, then his cheeks. 'Cam,' she groaned against him, and opened up her mouth, allowing him access to that sweet cavity.

Then her breasts were pressing against his chest, her stomach pushing into his. He saw her eyes widen as she realised his reaction to her, and under his mouth her lips felt as though they were smiling.

Cam placed his hands on the shapely backside that had been taunting him for days. She felt right, so soft yet firm.

The blasted phone rang.

Neither of them moved except to lift their mouths free of each other.

The phone continued ringing. Finally Cam

swore and stepped away to snatch the offending instrument from the counter. 'This had better be good. Hello?'

'Cam, Amanda. I'm just leaving with the boys. You've got five minutes.' Click and she'd gone.

'Do you have to go out?' Jenny asked.

Shaking his head, he felt laughter beginning to erupt. 'That was Amanda, warning us the boys are on their way home.'

A twinkle lit up her eyes. 'She's far too cheeky. But I guess we have to be grateful.'

'I think so.' That kiss could've been headed down the hall to his bedroom.

CHAPTER ELEVEN

AT FIVE JENNY gave up all pretence of sleeping and got up to pull on a sweatshirt and shorts. In the kitchen she made a mug of tea and took it outside, where she sat on the deck and watched the sun coming up from behind the hill on the other side of the estuary. As the sky lightened a sense of acceptance flowed over her.

She was going to have to tell Cam what had happened that day Alison had died. Their relationship would stall if she didn't. Last night's kiss told her there was a relationship on offer if she wanted it. She did. If Cam could see past her mistakes. If she could forgive herself.

Too many ifs.

How about another one? What if her feelings for Cam were love? It had to be. It gripped her, squeezed her heart, made her smile, laugh and sometimes cry. If that wasn't love, what was it?

Clink. A cup rattled against another in the kitchen. Cam was also up and about.

Sipping her tea, she waited for him to join her. Had he tossed and turned all night like she had? Even in the half-light his face showed signs of lack of sleep. 'Hey,' she whispered as he sat down in the chair next to her, holding his mug between those same firm hands that had gripped her bottom last night and set her hormones to dancing.

But the sleepless night, this drinking tea out here so early, was only half the problem. 'I have to be in the Kahurangi National Park on the thirteenth.'

She watched him raise the mug to those lips she wanted more of, saw his throat swallow, then heard him say, 'I'll drive you.'

'Just like that?' With no questions asked, he'd drive all that way for her?

'Yes.'

'It's a work day.'

'I'm owed time off.'

Those tears that she'd managed to hold onto all night spilled over and ran down her cheeks. 'Thank you.'

'No problem.'

The last quarter of the sun exploded over the horizon. The new day had arrived. Jenny drained her tea, set the mug on the floor, dug deep for strength, and told him, 'We were hiking along a cliff face. There was a track there, not well maintained but a track.' She swallowed down on the bile rising in her throat. 'I insisted on going first, whereas she usually did. We even joked about me being the bossy twin for a change.'

Cam nodded. 'You blame yourself for that.'

She nodded. 'When I was halfway across the face the track simply fell out from under me. Alison shouted a warning but it came too late.' She swallowed. 'She clambered down the edge of the slip after me, yelling all the time to hold on, she was coming.' Sniffed. 'A boulder broke lose and bounced down the cliff. It clipped Alison's head, crushed her chest.'

Cam's hand enveloped hers. He stayed quiet, waiting as though they had all day if she needed it.

This was hard. Even after all this time. Alison's silence ricocheted around inside her head.

Her own fear blocked her throat, turned her mouth sour.

Cam's thumb stroked the back of her hand.

She hauled in some air. 'I screamed at her to move, to get up. She didn't. No movement at all. When I reached her she was unconscious. I couldn't save her. I had nothing with me to help her. My cellphone was smashed, as was the emergency locator beacon in her pack.' The words spewed out of her mouth now. 'It tore me apart to even think of leaving her while I went out to the road for help. Deep down I think I knew she wouldn't make it.'

'You weren't injured?'

'Hardly, in comparison. Scrapes and bruises, torn muscles. Nothing to hold me back.'

'You stayed anyway?'

'I couldn't leave her, my sister, my twin. She died in my arms an hour later. I'd never have raised help in time to save her so I was glad I hadn't left her alone. How awful would that be? Dying alone?' Her lungs forced the air out in one long huff.

Forget holding her hand, Cam now wrapped her in his arms and sat her on his lap. 'Shh,

Jenny, sweetheart.' His lips grazed her forehead and he rocked her.

After what seemed like a long time but probably wasn't she continued, 'With my foot in a cast I can't walk in to that place where it happened, but I have to be as close as I can get for the anniversary.'

'You want to say goodbye?'

'No.' Hardly. 'I want to say sorry, beg Alison's forgiveness.'

The rocking stopped and Cam locked eyes with her. 'Whatever for?'

'Because I couldn't save her.'

The truth dawned in his brown eyes all too quickly. Except he didn't put her aside in disgust, or even agree she'd failed. Instead he said, 'Tell me if I'm wrong, but you were supposed to save Alison after a boulder smashed her head?' There was nothing but bewilderment and concern in his gaze. No horror at her failure.

Didn't he get it? 'Yes, I was.' She shivered. 'I understand the reality of the situation and how no one would've been able to help her. But the other half of me, the half attached to Alison, doesn't.'

224 of FAMILY THIS CHRISTMAS

'Oh, sweetheart.' Cam shook his head and wrapped her tight in his arms again. This time he didn't rock back and forth, just settled further in the seat and held her. 'We'll go together to the park.' That's all he said as they sat there for nearly an hour.

Not one word of condemnation, nothing about her responsibilities not being met, just the promise that they would go there together.

Was it possible she might get through this? Have a life on the other side of this? She wouldn't know for a few days yet.

The trip, a few days later, was painfully quiet, and got quieter as the kilometres passed beneath their wheels. Cam kept a watch over Jenny as she drew in on herself, hunching her shoulders forward as the environs of Nelson and Tasman dropped behind and hills and mountains began filling their vision. Should he get her talking to alleviate some of that tension tightening her shoulders?

He couldn't make any of this better for her. He'd give everything he had except his boys to make it go easy for her, though in reality he understood she had to do this and if anything could make her feel more at ease it was getting through today. 'What's the plan? How far in are we going?'

'Since I can't walk the track, I figured the car park is going to be it. I might try walking a little way along the track but it is very uneven and narrow.' She swivelled in her seat to stare at him. Better than watching those mountains getting bigger and bigger? 'The rescue crews used the car park as a base to conduct the search for us. We'd written our trip intentions in the hut books all along the track and when we were a day late Search and Rescue swung into action.'

'How overdue were you?'

'Twenty-four hours. I waited with Alison, holding her to me.'

The hitch in her voice snagged his heart and he lifted one hand from the steering wheel to cover hers. 'You were incredibly brave.' Then and today. He slowed the vehicle. 'This the turn-off?'

'Yes.' Her cheeks had paled more than usual.

As soon as he'd taken the turn he slowed, then stopped and took her hand in his again.

A slight tremor shook her, while her skin had turned cold. 'Hey, sunshine, you're doing fine.' But she wasn't really. Why would she? This had to be extremely hard. 'I'm here, okay?'

Jenny stared around. 'How did I think I could do this on my own?' she asked in a whisper. Shoving the passenger door wide, she dropped to the ground and, hands on hips, stared up at the mountain range dominating the skyline.

After parking, Cam strolled across to stand behind her and pulled her slim body in against him. Wrapping his arms around her waist, he dropped his chin on top of her head. 'What do you have in mind now that you're here?' He'd piggyback her along the track if she wanted to go into the bush. Probably cripple him for ever but he'd do it.

As Jenny rubbed her hands up and down her arms she continued to gaze around. 'The sun was shining the day it happened. A hot, wind-less day that sapped our strength. But we were impervious to that, loving every step we took through the bush and out in the open, listening to and watching the fantails flitting from bush to branch as they stayed just ahead of us.'

'Did you start out from here?'

Shaking her head, she explained, 'No, we came from the west. We had arranged for friends to walk the track in the opposite direction and we met in the middle, swapped car keys with them. That saved a lot of manoeuvring of vehicles before starting out.'

'I guess it would.'

'Our packs were heavy with gear and wet-weather clothing. I remember complaining about the ache in my shoulders when we reached the first hut where we spent that night. Alison told me to harden up. Sympathy was never her strong point.'

Cam rubbed his chin back and forth across her head. 'You two do a lot of tramping in remote areas?'

'It was our escape from everyday stresses and tensions. Ever since Dad took us on an overnight tramp out of Dunedin when we were ten we were hooked. You couldn't stop us from throwing our packs on our backs and heading out to some hill or mountain. Later, when we were busy with our careers, it became our twin time. We'd go for a week and just be us.'

'Bet you miss that more than anything else.' She had been lucky to have that relationship with her sister. It's what he wanted Andrew and Marcus to always have, a rock in their lives for when the bad times cropped up. His sisters were close to him and he knew how important that had been when Margaret had walked out on him.

Twisting around to look directly at him, Jenny said, 'You're right. It felt as though I'd been sliced down the middle and half of every part of me was missing.'

Her eyes glittered and with his thumb he smudged away an errant tear. 'Your mojo.'

'Yeah.' She drew the word out, then astonishingly her mouth curved ever so slightly upwards. 'I totally bamboozled the boys with that, didn't I?'

'They're still trying to find it for you.'

'Truly?' The smile widened. 'They are great little guys. So caring and thoughtful. They get that from you, I'd say.'

'Of course.' Though to be fair, 'Margaret wasn't always selfish. She used to be the person who turned up on your doorstep with baking if you'd had a bad day, or she'd change an appointment so she could take you to yours when you got a flat tyre.' Funny how now with Jenny he could acknowledge that.

'No one's all bad. I'm glad you told me that. Do you still miss her?' Those green eyes bored into him.

'Not at all. Haven't for a long time. But I still get angry at how she treats the boys.' *I thought today was about you, not me.* 'Want to walk a bit? See how that ankle stands up to the track?'

Her eyes locked with his for so long he began to think she'd gone to sleep with her eyes open, until finally she ducked her chin. 'Yes. You will be there with me, won't you?' Then she sucked a breath. 'Tell me if I'm expecting too much of you.'

'You're not. Trust me.'

After slinging his day pack on his back and locking the car, Cam walked behind Jenny as they stepped along the rutted, root-bound track, holding his breath every time she stumbled, breathing a sigh of relief when she went on. She carried a bunch of pink and white peonies against her chest. Alison's favourite flowers, apparently. After nearly an hour they reached a knoll and sat on the trunk of a large fallen tree. Sweat beaded their brows and dampened their arms and throats.

'It's a hot one.' Cam dumped the pack, then stretched his legs to ease the tightness in his calves. 'I enjoyed that. How's the ankle?'

'It's telling me I'm an idiot and I'm ignoring it. But I guess this is as far as I should go. It's not as if I can make it to the first hut, let alone to where the accident happened.' She bent to remove her boot. 'I know I shouldn't take this off until we get back to the car but I hate standing around in wet boots.'

There'd been a stream where they hadn't been able to avoid wading through knee deep water. 'If we're stopping here for a bit, I'll do the same. We can put them on that log in the sun.'

Jenny looked around. 'I remember stopping here for a nut bar and a juice on the way out with the rescuers.'

Talk about a cue. Unzipping the pack, Cam retrieved two juices and some oat and blueberry muffins from the bakery. 'Will these suffice?' He grinned, feeling like one of his boys when they did something cool.

Her eyes widened and her shoulders relaxed for the first time all morning. 'Thank you. Again. I seem to be saying that a lot this morning.'

'You can quit any time you like. I'm here because I care, because I want to be with you today.' And every other day, but putting that out there had to wait for a more suitable time.

'Thanks.' Leaning closer, she kissed his cheek. Then kissed it again.

Breathing in her scent, citrus overlaid with good, honest sweat, sent a shaft of desire arrowing through him right to his gut and beyond. He loved this woman. And right now was so not the moment to be reacting to her like this. But how not to? Love had brought him to this mountainside with her. He turned, kissed her cheek, then gently grazed her lips with his, before pulling back and deliberately stabbing the end of the straw into the hole on the top of the juice box. 'Drink up. I've got lots of goodies in that bag.'

'Like what? You didn't bring a picnic?'

Had that been the wrong thing to do? Today of all days should he have made sandwiches and left it at that? No. Jenny might be facing her grief but she could celebrate having made it through the first year too. 'Yep. I had to make myself useful.'

'Thanks, again.'

'You're welcome.'

They sat quietly, not speaking, for a while. Then Cam heard a soft sniff and saw a flood of tears streaming down Jenny's pale face. 'Hey, sunshine, come here.' And once again he wrapped her up in his arms.

'I miss her so much.'

His hand rubbed circles on her tense back.

'I still should've been able to save her.'

Huh? He shook her ever so gently and put her away from him enough to be able to gaze into her eyes. 'Being a doctor doesn't automatically make you superwoman. There was nothing you could do.' She must've been in mental agony. His hands tightened on her back, his palms seeking the warmth that told him she was alive and well now. 'At least your parents didn't lose both of you that day.' He brushed his lips across her forehead before tucking her back against his chest.

'I never thought of it like that before. I've been too busy blaming myself. I suggested we climb in Kahurangi Park. I even chose the track that fell away beneath us and sent us to the bottom. But Alison was with me all the way.'

Silence fell again. Then, 'She's not here. I thought I might sense her presence if I came on the same route but I don't. I remember her laughing and talking nonstop, but it's like any memory—no more, no less.'

She pulled back and stared around. 'But she's with me. Always will be. She's in here.' Her hands crossed on her chest, between her breasts. When Jenny stood Cam remained where he was, ready if she needed him, but giving her the space and time to reflect on what she'd just come to understand. She hadn't lost Alison. She never would.

Picking up the peonies, she crossed the knoll and walked around the edge of the grassed area until something caused her to stop. Slowly she squatted to lay the flowers on a small punga fern log. 'Bye bye, sis. Be safe.'

Tears wet her face, dripped off her chin, but the tension of earlier had eased off. Finally she looked up and locked her gaze with his. 'I'm going to say it again. Thank you. When I landed in a heap outside your house I had no idea how you were going to change my life. You and your boys.'

'Maybe we didn't. Maybe you were ready for it and were already opening up to opportunities.' He added lightly, 'Maybe you wished that skateboard on you.'

'You gave me those opportunities.'

'Okay. I'll take all the credit if it makes you happy.' He felt a lightness settling over him that he hadn't known in a long time. 'If I'd known the changes you'd bring to my life I'd have paid Marcus a long time ago to run you down.'

'Cam, make love to me.' She stood in front of him, her hands reaching for his.

What? Had he heard correctly? Nah, couldn't have. Jenny wanted to make love? With him? Here? All reasoning vanished. Instead, that lightness he'd felt had turned to heat and tension, warming his blood, driving his hormones south. Unfolding himself from the trunk, he said, 'For the record, Alison definitely isn't here? She's not looking down on you? Us?'

Her smile was beautiful. Those deep emerald eyes twinkled out at him. 'No. This is a private party.' Her smile dipped. 'Not a party. But something I want to do with you. You're helping me move on. Making love will help further.' He must've shown disappointment because she quickly added, 'Truth? I've been fantasising about this for days.'

'You've been fantasising about having sex in the bush?'

Her smile wavered. 'Worded wrongly. It definitely wasn't a plan to ask you to make love out here.' He saw the uncertainty taking control of her stance as her shoulders slumped and her back curled forward. She was fragile, very fragile, and he loved her. Besides, he'd been dreaming of holding her naked and close since the first night she'd stayed in his house.

'I like it that you've been fantasising about me, because you've been drowning all coherent thought in my head for days.' He took her face in his hands and leaned closer to kiss her. Her lips trembled under his mouth. His breath hitched as he softened his kiss, not wanting to come on too hard, too fast. Yet his body was screaming for the taste of her, to feel her skin against his, to know her soft curves. He wanted to feel her hands on him, her tongue tracing a line from his nipple to his stomach and beyond. He needed to take this slowly, let Jenny relax into their lovemaking and forget for a while why she'd come to this remote place.

'Jenny, wait. We have to stop. You have to believe me when I say that I want to make love to you more than anything in this world right now, but I wasn't expecting this. I'm not prepared. Hell, I don't even have any protection at home. Haven't needed it for years now. Since long before Margaret...'

Jenny tugged him closer. 'Cam, it's fine. I'm on the Pill. Not that I've needed to be since my last relationship ended, but now I'm so glad I kept filling that prescription.' She smiled cheekily before pressing her mouth against his. She had to taste him. Now. When her tongue slid into his mouth she shivered. Delicious. This was Cam. The man who'd stolen her heart when she hadn't even known if she'd still had one. Now she wanted to know him completely, nothing between them. Today had been hard. So damn hard, yet he'd been there for her, with her, and somehow it had been easier. And now this. This felt right. This was about the future, not the past year.

Cam's body was firm where his thighs pressed hers, where his chest covered her breasts, where his stomach touched hers. And further down the ridge pressing against her told her how much he wanted her. Slipping a hand between them, she reached down, ran her fingertips over the fabric-covered bulge.

Cam gasped, tipped his head back to lock eyes with her. On tiptoe she followed him, her mouth hungry for his, hating the brief break from their kiss. When his hands slid under her shirt and skimmed over her skin she thought she'd died and gone to heaven, except she felt far too alive. Hot need poured through her, swelling up and out from her heart, filling every cell of her body. Drenching her. Yes, she was ready for Cam.

Snatching handfuls of his shirt, she jerked upwards, pulling it free of his bush pants. At least the pants had an elastic waistband and easily slid over those firm hips when she pushed them down. And then he was free, filling her hands; the whole, hot, pulsating length of him.

She wanted him, right now, inside her. 'Undress me,' she hissed through clenched jaws.

'You don't want to take your time?' he croaked, even as his hands were scrabbling at her belt buckle.

'I've wasted weeks already.' Her hand slid down the length that was turning her to liquid just with the slick feel of him. 'Cam, can we do this now?' Like right now?

'Help me out here,' he begged. Her belt finally gave way and Cam's hot hands were on her hips, pushing her trousers down. Over her thighs, down to her knees.

Reaching down, she tugged first one then the other leg free of clothing. Then she proceeded to divest him of his trousers.

Cam swung her up in his arms and knelt to lay her on the grass. Quickly grabbing him, she hauled him down to cover her, opening for him. 'Cam, I—' *Love you.* The words were lost on a haze of heat and desire as he pressed into her. Instinctively her hips lifted to receive him. She moved beneath him, making it impossible for him to hold back. And then she succumbed to the oblivion that her release brought.

* * *

Cam had made her whole again. By being with her today, by claiming her body so thoroughly. By being Cam, gentle, tough, kind and loving. Jenny held his sweat-slicked body close. When he made to move off her, she tightened her grip. 'I like your weight on me.' Even if he was making breathing difficult. 'I never want to let you go.'

With a wriggle Cam managed to tug his arms free and rose on his elbows to gaze down at her. His face was flushed and his eyes still held that molten look that had turned her on so thoroughly. 'I'm not going anywhere without you.' His hand brushed her hair off her forehead and cheek. 'Besides, I owe you long and slow.'

A laugh began deep inside her, tripped up her throat and spilled between them. 'Long and slow, eh?'

'Yeah, you know, when I get to touch every part of your delectable body with my tongue? When you're crying out for me to give you what you want? That long and slow.' His grin was wicked and, oh, so sexy.

'I can't wait.'

'I've never taken you for being so impatient. Where's the quiet, controlled Jenny gone?'

'I save her for rainy days. And right now the sun's shining.'

Cam kissed her softly on her now tender lips before slowly sliding off her and sitting up. 'I've got just the thing for sunny days.' When he pulled a wine cooler out of his backpack she gaped.

'You carried a bottle of wine up here?'

'Not any old wine, but this.' With a flourish he tugged the bottle free of the tight cooling bag. 'Champagne.'

'If I hadn't already told you enough times already, I'd say thank you.'

He unwrapped two champagne flutes then popped the cork. 'The best sound in the world.'

'Quickly followed by the fizz and sizzle of bubbles as you pour that into those glasses.' Shuffling on her bottom, she pulled her trousers up to her waist but didn't bother to zip them closed. Who knew what might happen after a glass of champagne?

CHAPTER TWELVE

MARCUS AND ANDREW, followed by two of their friends, raced out the front door of Amanda's house the moment Cam turned into her driveway. 'You're back.'

'Whoopee, we can go home.'

Jenny shoved her door open and stepped down. Wow, she was tired, and that was after sleeping most of the way from Kahurangi. 'I wasn't scintillating company.' She gave Cam a wry smile.

She didn't hear his answer as the boys all but leapt at her. 'Jenny, you came back.'

'We thought you were gone for ever.'

Jenny's heart stuttered, and guilt forced her to glance at Cam, who was watching his boys with a very guarded expression on his face. 'Of course we were coming back. I told you we would.'

'Me, too.' Amanda and some more children

joined their group. 'Jenny, you okay?' She knew a little about where they'd been for the day.

Nodding slowly, Jenny sought for an answer, but what the twins had said had rocked her off centre—when she'd only just got back there after all this time. Marcus and Andrew had thought she wouldn't be coming back, which meant they'd believed she was staying on for a while—or longer.

Cam filled the sudden gap in the conversation. 'It's been a long day. Thanks so much for looking after the boys, Amanda.' His brow furrowed as he looked from Jenny to his sons and back again. He wasn't happy.

She didn't blame him. Right from the outset she'd known he didn't want his boys getting hurt.

Marcus nudged one of his friends. 'I told you we're getting a new mother. We've seen Dad kissing her.'

The abrupt silence was only broken when Cam snapped, 'Marcus, Andrew, get in the truck. Now.'

Amanda gave Jenny a swift hug. 'Come and see me tomorrow. We'll have coffee.'

Tomorrow. A whole new day. It should be a

blank canvas for her to decide her next moves, but the twins had shown her that was not possible. She had to go before they became even more attached to her. All she could hope for was that she hadn't done any permanent damage, staying as long as she had.

The boys went straight to bed and Jenny headed for the shower to wash away the day—the sweat, the sex, the exhaustion. When she came out wrapped in her sleeping T-shirt and an oversized robe of Cam's, he had mugs of tea waiting.

'Cam, about the boys—'

'It's been a long, emotional day. Let's talk about that tomorrow.'

The problem was tomorrow never seemed to come for her.

Did Cam want time to think about what he would say to her? How he'd explain she had to go for his sons' sakes? *Believe me, Cam, I get it. I am going. This time I mean it.*

For some inexplicable reason she couldn't stop watching his hands as they held his cup and lifted it to his mouth. Those hands had made love to her. She'd wanted to know them on her body once, just once. And now she had. Twice. Only twice wasn't enough. Not by any measure she could think of.

But she'd have to make do with the memories of that afternoon. That's all she'd have. No opportunity to make more beautiful mental pictures for later. She couldn't stay, not even that long. She wasn't the boys' mother, yet right now they'd fitted her into the slot as a replacement.

When she'd first arrived, Andrew and Marcus had been desperate to find Margaret and have her back in their lives. Jenny accepted there was no way the role was hers. She couldn't replace their mum. They wanted, needed, far more than she had to give. Yes, she loved them. More importantly, she loved their father. But she couldn't do what they wanted. Because one day she might fail them and they'd say, 'You're not our mother. You can't tell us what to do, or how to do it. It's not your place.' Cam would be forced to stand up for them, and she'd be broken-hearted again.

Hang on. Wasn't she jumping the gun here? Cam had probably never intended for her to stay on past getting her foot out of plaster—if that long. It wasn't as though he'd come out declaring his love for her. She'd been overlaying everything he'd done and said with her own love, not realising Cam hadn't been at the same game.

So she went for damage control, and told Cam, 'Today I put Alison's death in perspective. I know now it wasn't my fault.' This was way harder than she'd ever have believed. It went to show how much she loved Cam. 'But...' *get on with it* '...just as importantly, staying with you has given me so much. I've started to find myself again.' Her mojo.

'But here's the rub. I'm not sure yet what my future holds for me. I can't make promises that involve you or your family. I won't guarantee I'll stay around once I finally get myself sorted. I don't even know if I want to return to an ED. Or medicine in any form. And if I don't do that, who am I?' She'd wanted to be a doctor since Donny Browning had stubbed his toe at her third birthday party. Yet knowing she hadn't been able to save her twin hadn't stopped her confidence being undermined enough to terrify her.

'What about that wee girl in the Wairau ED? You saved her life.' Thoughtful brown eyes locked with her gaze.

'Instinct. I didn't stop to think.' She held her hand up. 'And before you say that proves I've still got it medically, it's not the same as making hard decisions about how to treat someone when the situation isn't as urgent.'

'I could mention Amanda, little Lily or Haydon. You were great with them, too.' Cam drained his cup and leaned forward, his elbows on his knees. 'Don't you think it's time to let this go? Be kind to yourself. Forgive yourself.'

He'd missed the point. 'This isn't about guilt now. This is about not knowing who I am any more. I am beginning to think I might return to medicine but I'm nowhere near certain. Until I work that out I can't stay here. It isn't fair on you, and it especially isn't fair on your boys. What if I take off after a few weeks? Or months even? It's going to hurt them and you're already dealing with their mother having let them down.'

She knew Cam didn't get how she could be contemplating giving up medicine for ever. It would be a rare doctor who did. It took so much hard work to qualify, not to mention a ton of dedication, that rarely did anyone ever consider walking away. Tears pricked the backs of her eyelids. Unfortunately, when she opened her mouth there were no more words. She wanted to tell Cam she loved him, and his boys. But she'd still have to say she was leaving so it was probably best she'd become mute.

But the pain. It lanced her, sliced her heart to shreds, twisted her stomach so tight she thought she'd be ill. She should never have stopped here for more than that first night. But it had been too easy to put off leaving. Cam made her feel almost whole again. He'd done more for her in a few short weeks then she'd done all year actively searching for her life.

'The boys still keep looking for your mojo.' Cam's face was sad. 'Though I think you've found some of it already.'

She nodded, slowly drew in air to her lungs and spoke softly. 'I know. But, Cam, they have to stop. I can't complete my side of the bargain.' Not that she'd actually agreed to help find their mother for them. The boys had taken her willingness for granted. 'You have to talk to them about their mother. I can't.'

'You're right.' His smile was rueful and brief, and added to her sadness.

She'd lost Alison suddenly. Losing Cam was going to be slow and difficult. But the pain would be similar. Strange, considering she'd loved Alison since the day they were born, and yet had only known Cam for little more than two weeks.

Cam stood up, stretching his arms above his head. 'We're both tired. Go to bed. We'll talk again tomorrow.'

She should pack her few belongings and hitch a ride out of Havelock right now. But Cam was right about one thing. She was exhausted, emotionally as well as in every muscle in her body. Hopefully she'd manage some sleep tonight.

Cam watched Jenny trudge down the hall to the room that had become hers. Half of him wanted to follow and crawl into bed beside her, hold her tight, and maybe even make love again. Though that exhaustion pulling at her probably precluded any activity tonight. Just holding her would be fine. He could stroke that soft, satin-like skin, breathe in her scent of lemon and lime.

Rinsing out their mugs, he turned to stare at new photos of Andrew and Marcus pinned to the noticeboard. They stood either side of Jenny, grinning at him as he took the picture out on the lawn, looking so happy. Happier than he'd known them to be for so long he'd begun to wonder if they'd ever know happiness again. Jenny had done that for them.

She could easily break their little hearts by taking off again. Tomorrow might be the day. Or it could be in a month's time. Or a year's. As much as he wanted to believe he could keep her content here with him, an element of doubt picked at his thinking. Jenny was restless. Today's trip hadn't changed that after all. As she'd been direct in pointing out. So, if she was leaving, the sooner the better for his boys.

His heart ached. She'd not only helped the boys, she'd changed his outlook on life. He had a spring in his step, he felt hope for the future again. He could almost taste it: the complete family he'd always wanted, the holidays, showing the boys the way through life's obstacles. Jenny would be perfect for him. He knew that without a doubt.

But bottom line—he couldn't risk the boys being hurt again. Margaret had a lot to answer for. He would not compound their anguish by making a mistake with Jenny. No matter what the cost to him and his heart. He came second in this small family.

Tonight he didn't need to make a mental note about anything, he wouldn't be sleeping anyway. He'd be wide awake, rueing the day that skateboard had smacked into Jenny's ankle and tumbled her into their lives. In a matter of weeks he'd found his soulmate, a woman he loved more than he'd have believed possible. Yet tomorrow he'd talk to her and then, he suspected, he'd watch her walk away. It was the only answer for his boys.

But he had one more thing to ask—make that demand—of her before she walked out the door for the last time.

'You mustn't leave without saying goodbye to Andrew and Marcus.' Cam stepped into the kitchen as Jenny squeezed the teabag and dumped it in the trash can.

Knowing he'd join her out here as soon as the sun began making its appearance, she still gasped with surprise. He'd moved so quietly through the house she hadn't even heard a floorboard creak. Had he been standing there, watching her? Thinking of yesterday or of tomorrow? Forget those days. She had today to get through.

'Jenny.' She'd never heard him sound so harsh, not even when the boys exasperated him. 'It's not space tripping you do, is it? It's avoidance. When my questions get too tough you pretend you didn't hear me.'

Another gasp. 'I've answered more questions this past fortnight than I have in a year. I've told you way more about me and my screwed-up life than I've talked to anyone else about it.' She should've sneaked out in the middle of the night, phoned for a taxi to come out from Blenheim to pick her up. The coward's way out. Easier on her heart. Easier on Cam and his boys. Instead, she'd waited out the long, long hours of darkness so she could see Cam one last time. But there weren't going to be any happy thank-you-very-much-have-a-great-life farewells this morning. That was apparent in his strained face, in those tired brown eyes watching her every breath.

He snapped his fingers in front of her face. 'Hello? Just this once give me your full, un-divided attention. I want you to explain to the twins that you're heading away and why. I do not want them thinking they've done something bad that's made you go.'

He was in full protect-his-sons mode, and for that she admired him. Nodding her agreement, she said, 'I will make sure they understand this has nothing to do with them.' Picking up her mug in less than steady hands, she gripped it tight and clumped across to the sliding glass door leading out onto the deck. Might as well sit out the next couple of hours, watching the sun crawling ever higher, while trying to come up with something appropriate to say to Marcus and Andrew that they'd understand.

By the time the boys bounced outside to shout good morning she was none the wiser about how to handle the situation. Her mind had been focused entirely on the man she was leaving behind. Cameron had been responsible for her new, improved outlook on life. He'd made her feel again. And feeling led back to hurting. This time the pain was self-inflicted.

'Jenny, you haven't forgotten the carols on the marina next week, have you?' Andrew stood directly in front of her.

Her heart dropped to her stomach.

Marcus added, 'You will wear that Santa's hat I made specially, won't you?'

Nausea raced up her throat. Slapping a hand over her mouth, she dug deep to keep her stomach from tossing her tea at the twins' feet. Twisting her head from side to side, she waited until she knew her voice box would work in some semblance of normal.

'Why's your bag on the step?' Marcus asked.

Andrew spun around to see what his brother was talking about, spun back. 'Where are you going? Can we come?'

Cam cleared his throat. 'Boys, Jenny has to go home today.'

Gratitude for his intervention was instantly replaced by remorse. He sounded like he was talking through a waterfall, all distorted and deep. She opened her mouth, tentatively tried to speak. 'I'm so sorry, Andrew, Marcus.' Her mouth snapped shut. Try again. That's not enough. Her chest rose as she breathed deep.

'It's time for me to go home.' Now, there was a lie. She didn't have a home. This house had been as close as she'd been to having a home for so long that nowhere else seemed right. As the boys' mouths opened to state the inevitable, she quickly continued. 'I only stayed while my ankle got better. Now I have to find a job and go and see my parents.' Suddenly that left field idea seemed the right thing to do. Go back to Dunedin and mend some bridges with Mum and Dad before deciding where she'd go next.

'But we don't—'

'Want you to go.'

Tears tracked down two small, dismayed faces. Tears that broke her heart all over again. 'I have to.' One day they'd see she'd done the right thing by them. Reaching forward, she dragged the boys into a hug. But they weren't having any of that. They pulled free and ran to stand beside Cam.

'Tell her, Dad.'

'She can't go.'

He placed a hand on each boy's shoulder. 'Sorry, guys, but Jenny is going.' The eyes that locked with hers chilled her right to the bone.

Standing, she made it to the step and hoisted her bag over her shoulder. Clumping down to the path, she tried to walk away without looking back, but her feet seemed glued to the concrete. Turning, she looked up at Cam, devouring every line of his beautiful face, storing images in her head for those long, lonely nights that would become a part of her life again. 'Goodbye, Cam. Goodbye, Marcus. Goodbye, Andrew.' If her heart hadn't already broken into a million pieces back there on the deck, it would've completely vaporised now.

At the corner of their street Cam hugged his boys to him and cursed Jenny for their tears. Andrew and Marcus had insisted they wave to Jenny as the bus went past, but there hadn't been any answering wave from inside the vehicle as it had sped by. Had she deliberately ignored them? Or had she sat on the far side so she wouldn't know if they'd come to see her off?

'Come on, guys. Let's go home.'

The bus slowed and he held his breath. Had Jenny changed her mind? Would the door open and Jenny hop out, yelling she'd made a mistake and asking if he'd let her stay on? *Yeah, and what would your answer be?* Because if she stayed the possibility of rerunning this scene would always be there. Jenny couldn't commit. *Oh, and you can? Did you once tell her how you feel about her?* Despite the heat in the day already cranking up, Cam shivered. He was looking out for his kids. *Excuses, excuses.*

A dog ran across the road in front of the bus. The bus sped up. Jenny hadn't stopped the driver. A damned dog had.

'Breakfast-time then you can get ready for school and the class picnic.' He nudged the boys towards home.

'I don't want to go.' Andrew stamped his foot.

'It won't be fun without Jenny.' Marcus added his say.

You're not wrong there, my boy. 'We'll make it fun, our fun, like we always have.' Ouch. That was it, really. They'd been full circle and were now back to where they'd been a couple of weeks ago. The three of them. 'It's the last week of the term, remember? That's got to be good.'

Disbelief at his statement blinked out at him from two identical pairs of eyes. 'Yes, Dad.' Their voices were flat, beaten.

His heart crunched. Damn it. Jenny had won him over without even trying. Hard to believe how easily, in fact. 'We won't be beaten.' Neither boy understood what he meant but he did. 'Let's go. We'll have pancakes with syrup.' He'd clean up the resulting mess tonight.

'Yes, Dad.' At least there was some enthusiasm in their voices this time. Some was better than none. Just.

Note to self: keep my boys busy so that they don't get too gloomy over Jenny's leaving.

Second note to self: keep myself busy so that I don't get too gloomy over Jenny's leaving.

Note to self: ignore all notes to myself.

Since watching Jenny's bus roll through Havelock, Cam had been through one of the longest weeks of his life.

Getting Jenny out of his head, out of his system, had proved to be impossible. He missed her so much it was agony.

So call her. Tell her exactly that.

Sure. That would work—until she left again. The boys weren't coping, moping around the place like someone had stolen their favourite toys. Hell, not even Christmas, only days away, was exciting them.

'Dad…'

'Yes?' Cam clipped the lids on the boys' lunch-boxes and glanced at his watch. He'd forgotten to make the lunches last night after getting home from having dinner with Amanda and her family. Forgotten. That never happened.

'Did Jenny find her mojo?' Andrew stared up at him.

He suspected that was the last thing she'd found after all. 'I don't think so, guys.'

'If we keep looking and find it, will she come back?'

'We miss her.'

Me, too. He cleared his throat. 'Me, too.' More than he'd have believed. 'Jenny has lots of things worrying her at the moment.'

'Did you ask her to stay?' Andrew kicked the stool.

'No.' *I was afraid of hurting you both further down the track.* 'Guys, you have to understand you can't make a person stay if they don't want to.'

'How do you know she didn't want to if you didn't ask her?'

Since when had Marcus got so smart? 'I…'

I don't know. Jenny was adamant she had to go and I was adamant I had to protect you two so I never considered asking if there was some way we could get around her problems and make it work for all of us.

'But where will she have Christmas?'

'At school we made her a box to put her mojo in when she finds it. We don't want her to lose it again.'

'Can we wrap it in Christmas paper?'

Cam sat down hard on the stool. They'd made a box for Jenny. So they hadn't given up on her returning.

You have. You gave up before she even left. Same as when Margaret wanted to go find herself. Back then you put the boys first and let her break your heart. Exactly what you've done again. Only this time it feels as though you've lost more than the mother of your children. It feels—feels like half of you has disappeared.

'A box is a cool idea, guys. We'll find a way to get it to her.'

I'll make sure of that, and maybe I could put my heart in it so she knows what she means to me.

After the boys were tucked up for the night Cam sat down with his cell and pressed Jenny's number. His gut tightened as he listened to her voice-mail. Her soft southern lilt tore him apart. When the message ended he pressed redial, listened again, and left a message, asking her to call.

An hour later when his phone hadn't rung and he'd checked a dozen times to make sure the battery wasn't flat, he tapped his computer to life and sent her an email.

Hey, there, wondering how you're doing? The boys are on countdown to Christmas. They...

He tapped backspace four times.

We miss you.
Hugs, Cam, Andrew and Marcus.

At one o'clock he gave up pretending she would answer and dragged himself off to bed. In the morning he'd try again.

Same result.

Lunchtime—same result.

Cam came to a decision. He wanted Jenny back in his life. He'd risk everything, even rejection, to achieve that, would fight with every-thing he had to win her back.

Dearest Jenny.

I love you. I think I have from the moment I found you sprawled on the path at my gate. If the way my heart went crazy is an indicator then yes, I did. You looked so beautiful, even when your face was contorted with pain. I wanted to run my hands through that silken hair spilling every-where. I couldn't take your pain away but believe me, if I could have, I would have. I didn't want to ask you to stay with us but I couldn't stop myself. You were already weaving your way into my soul. I wanted to get to know you, to share some time with you, to laugh and talk together.

And now I have, I miss you so much. It's like someone took a chainsaw and cut me down the middle. I'm not complete.

You're fun, serious, genuine, caring. You even started learning to cook—for us.

Cam hesitated, wiped the sweat off his brow.

There's a place for you here, by my side, in my life and heart, with my sons. There's a niche for

you in Havelock, too, if the number of times people stop me to ask after you is a clue. Can you
find it in your heart to return? To join us? To join
me? For ever?

I understand how difficult life has been for you
since the accident that took Alison's life. I'd like
to help you continue to get on your feet. I'm prepared to chance it that you might one day wake
up and realise you'd made a mistake and leave us.

Another swipe at his brow. This baring his
soul wasn't easy. But at least he was trying, and
it was a little easier than it would be to say these
things out loud to her.

Jenny, I love you. Please come home.

Click. Send.

For a long time he sat staring at the computer,
willing his heart rate to slow to normal. He'd
done it, told Jenny everything he felt, and now
all he could do was wait. She might never answer, but he had given his all and tried.

'Dad, we're bored.'

'Now, there's something new.' Cam unfolded
from the chair and stood up. He had the after-

noon off. Spending time doing something with the boys would help pass the hours until he could hope to get a reply from Jenny. 'Okay, guys, let's go get our Christmas tree from the pine forest.'

'Yeah.'

'Cool.'

At least he'd made them happy about something.

CHAPTER THIRTEEN

CAM STARED AT the Christmas tree standing in its pot in the corner of the lounge, decorated so heavily only the pine scent and some fallen needles gave a clue to the type of tree it was. The boys had gone overboard in their enthusiasm for hanging baubles and velvet reindeer pulling miniature sleighs. Each had tried to outdo the other with their creativity. When they'd finished they'd placed the one parcel in the house that was ready to go underneath the branches.

A present for Jenny. The box they'd lovingly put together and painted at school.

Cam could feel his heart breaking all over again. Jenny had stolen three hearts in this household.

Well, there was nothing he could do about Jenny right now. If he didn't hear from her soon he might have to resort to tracking her parents down in Dunedin and try coercing her where-abouts out of them. He wouldn't give up in a hurry that was for sure.

He glanced at his watch and groaned. Might as well prepare dinner. In the kitchen Cam stared at the mince defrosting on the bench. His mouth soured. Mince. Patties. Same old, same old. Just the thought of cooking turned his stomach.

'Can we have fish and chips tonight?' Marcus had to be on the same wavelength. 'I'm sick of patties.'

'Why not? I'll phone Diane and put in an order.' Decision made, as easy as that.

'Can we go and get them?'

'On our own?'

'Sure.' The shop was only four hundred me-tres away and it wasn't as though Havelock was a den of iniquity. Kids were always visiting the shops. 'Let me phone first.'

While the boys were away Cam started to clear away the clutter that had accumulated over the day. One day he might manage to train the boys to put things away as they finished with them. Maybe.

Jenny had seemed to get them to do things so

easily. Had she been a novelty? Had they been trying to impress her to stay?

Round and round went the questions that had no answers. *Where are you, Jenny? Dunedin? Or back on the road, this time in a bus, stopping wherever?* She still had to collect her car someday, and hopefully he'd be around when she did. There again, after that email she might wait until he was working at the Blenheim clinic before dropping by here.

'To hell with this.' Tossing two pairs of sports shoes in the shoe basket in the laundry, he headed for the fridge and an ice-cold beer. Out on the deck he sipped from the bottle and stared around his empty yard, and cringed. There was nothing wrong with Havelock, his home or his family. But there had to be more to life. A life with Jenny in it for starters. 'Where is she?'

The front door crashed open. 'Dad, got the fish and chips.' The boys bundled out on to the deck. Then, 'We saw Jenny in the bakery.'

His heart stopped. The bottle of beer fell from a lifeless hand. It was happening all over again. But this time the apparition Marcus and Andrew were seeing was Jenny. Not their mother. Pain and shock slammed through him, kicked at his heart, made it pound against his ribs and send deafening thuds to his ears. Shaking his head, he held his arms out to the twins. 'No. No, you didn't. Jenny's gone. You have to accept that.'

'No, Dad. She hasn't.'

'It's true. We saw her.'

This was bad. How did he make them understand that no matter how hard they tried they couldn't wish anyone they wanted back into their lives? His chest rose as his lungs filled with much-needed oxygen.

'They're not making me up. I am here.'

The air whooshed out of his lungs. His head spun round so fast he felt giddy. 'Jenny? Is that really you?' Who else had red hair that made the day so bright? Who else had such a sweet, heart-melting smile that warmed him to his toes? What other woman could look so beautiful while looking apprehensive? 'Jenny.'

'I got your email.'

Suddenly—who knew how?—he was in front of this woman who'd stolen his heart and reaching for her, covering her mouth with his. Words were beyond him.

When her hands locked at the back of his neck and her breasts pressed against his chest, he prayed that this was true, that he hadn't taken to seeing and feeling apparitions the same way his sons did. Pulling his head back, he stared into those suck-him-in green eyes that had swamped his dreams every night since that day she'd landed in his life. 'You came.' For him? Them all? Then a shocking idea struck. For her car?

But she still had that cast on, was wearing the biggest, brightest smile he'd ever seen, and her eyes were full of—? Love? For him? And, if he needed more convincing, hadn't she kissed him back a moment ago?

'Yes, Cameron, I came back. That email choked me up. You never said a tenth of any of that when I said I was going.'

'I'm not good at verbalising.'

She just grinned at him. 'I know. A real man doesn't say he loves a woman, he shows her. I should've read the manual before I left. But then again I didn't tell you how much I love you either.'

He started to lean closer to that delectable

mouth again, but it seemed Jenny hadn't finished.

'You also reiterated what I'd already begun to see for myself. I was running from the best thing that had ever happened to me—you and the boys. A family. A man who loves me regardless of what I've been or who I'll become. A man who had the patience and love to help me through last week and to open my eyes to more than I believed I deserved.'

Then I got it right. The sweat and pain had been worth every drop, and then some. 'Seems you don't have any trouble telling me what's on your mind.' Covering her mouth, he shut up any more words she might have lurking in there. He'd heard what he needed to hear for now. Jenny was back.

'Dad, is Jenny staying?'

'Jenny, will you do some more cooking? I'm sick of patties.'

'And sausages.'

'Can you stay for Christmas?'

This kiss just wasn't going to happen any time soon. Cam shoved a hand through his hair and grinned at Jenny and his boys. 'This is family life. No privacy. Plenty of interruptions. Think you can handle it full time?'

'Try and stop me.'

'Good answer.'

Marcus high-fived his brother. 'She's staying. What night of the week do we want beef stroganoff?'

Jenny laughed. 'What about meat patties night?' Hopefully Amanda would help her get past the lasagne and beef stroganoff and then every meal would be a surprise.

'No, that's fish and chip night now.'

'Dad, the fish and chips are getting cold.'

'Then go and eat them.' He hadn't taken his gaze away from Jenny. 'You hungry?'

Shaking her head, she laughed again. 'Not yet. But a glass of wine would go down a treat. You want to replace that beer you managed to spill everywhere?'

'Yes.' Finally he looked around, then back to Jenny, and felt a well of emotion back up in his throat. 'Thank you for returning. I had decided I'd chase you down if you didn't.'

'I went home, spent two days with Mum and Dad. We talked a lot about Alison and the accident. I guess we had the conversations we should've had twelve months ago.'

'It would've been harder back then. You've had time to come to terms with your loss, as have your parents.'

Her smile softened. 'They were great. I told them all about you and the boys. They can't wait to meet you.'

'Hang on.' Cam looked at her more closely. 'Were you intending to come and see us? I didn't need to email you?'

Her laugh scared the sparrows off the lawn, where the boys were feeding them chips. 'Don't think you could get off that lightly. But, seriously...' Her laughter quietened. 'Putting things into perspective with Mum and Dad made me think about you and me. I flew back yesterday and immediately went to see Angus, who put me in contact with the head of the ED at Wairau.'

Cam held his breath. This was happening too fast. The fact she'd come back to him had only just started sinking in and she was talking about the hospital.

Running the back of her hand down his cheek, she said, 'Starting the first of February I'm working three days a week in the ED. I turned down full-time hours. I want to be a part of your lives, not living on the perimeter—which means there'll be cooking lessons, a house to run and three demanding males to keep in order. I think my life's going to be quite hectic.'

That emotion backing up finally spilled over. Tears rolled down his cheeks, laughter bubbled over his lips. 'Welcome home.'

Home. One tiny word that filled Jenny with warmth and love. She looked around the yard and sighed. One day soon she'd begin digging a garden and planting her favourite flowers so there'd always be colour out here.

Home. Who'd have thought she'd end her travels in Havelock? 'What do you reckon, Alison? Have I done the right thing or what?' Alison would be happy for her. She knew that bone deep. All either of them had wanted was for the other to find love and be happy.

'Here, get your lips around this.' Cam handed her a glass of bubbles. 'We're celebrating.'

She laughed. 'I'm glad this is a celebration.'

'Jenny, have you seen our tree?'

'Dad took us to the forest and cut a big pine.'

'We decorated it today.'

'Come and see it.'

She tapped the rim of her glass against Cam's. 'I know an order when I hear one.'

Cam took her hand and walked inside. 'Boys, quieten down a bit, will you?'

Jenny stopped in front of the tree. 'Wow, look at that. You've both done a fabulous job of decorating it. I've never seen so many decorations in my life.'

'We are allowed to buy three new ones each every year.'

'We haven't got them this year yet.'

She blinked. Where would they put them? 'When are you going shopping?'

'Tomorrow.'

'Can we, Dad?'

'I can't see why not.' Cam looked at her. 'Up for a bout in the shops?'

'Absolutely. I can't wait.'

'You have no idea what you're letting yourself in for.' His grin was wicked.

She nodded. 'Yes, I have. I'm going with my favourite males to load up on presents. What more could a woman want?' It would be like a family outing. Warmth flooded her. How had she thought she could walk away? This past week had been hell, and here she was, back where she now knew she belonged.

'Dad, we're going to be late for the carols.'

Cam's eyes widened and he tapped his forehead. 'Blame Jenny. She sidetracked me.'

'Carols? As in singing and holding candles?' When was the last time she'd done that?

'Yep, down at the marina. Coming with us?' Cam seemed to be holding his breath.

'Be warned, if I sing everyone will leave.'

'We'll take that chance. It would mean we can come home earlier anyway.'

If she'd thought he'd looked wicked before she'd been wrong. Now he looked very wicked. Her stomach flipped at the thought of what they might be doing after they came home. After they'd packed the boys off to bed, of course.

The marina was crowded. Everyone in Havelock and from the outlying bays must have come. The boys bounced around with excitement. Then they found Amanda's kids and dragged Cam and Jenny across to join them all.

Amanda gave her a hug. 'Glad you're home.'

'Was I the only one not to realise this is where I belong?' She hugged her friend back.

'I wouldn't have taken you for a slow learner but that goes to show how little I know.'

'It means you've got a cookery pupil for quite some time.'

Amanda chuckled. 'Guess I'll cope. We'll start with fruit mince tarts this week.'

'Perfect.'

'Here, better be lighting our candles.' Cam handed her and the boys a candle each then lit them. 'Marcus, Andrew, be careful with these. I don't want anybody getting burnt.'

'Yes, Dad.'

'Yes, Dad.'

Jenny laughed. Wasn't she doing a lot of that today? 'Yes, Cam.' She loved it when the boys looked so solemn. It wouldn't last. Any moment now they'd be joining in the singing and would forget every word Cam had said, but that was okay, because she'd be right here keeping an eye on them, along with their dad.

Cam leaned close, his breath warm on her cheek. 'I love Christmas mince tarts.'

'Yeah, but will the boys? Amanda? Can I get a recipe off you? I've got an idea.'

'As long as you promise not to tell everyone you got it from me.' Her friend grinned.

'Make it a very simple recipe, Amanda. Something with no more than two ingredients.' Cam added his two cents' worth.

'I'll surprise the lot of you.' She pulled a face at them both. 'You'll see.'

Cam handed Jenny another present to place under the tree, and told her, 'When I was the boys' age I used to get up early every morning and check out the presents under the tree, counting how many were for me then shaking and squeezing them trying to figure out what they were.'

Yeah, she had those memories, too. 'Whenever Mum was out Alison and I used to search under the window seat for parcels that could be our presents. It never spoilt the fun of opening them on Christmas morning, did it?' She began emptying the carton of neatly wrapped presents she'd bought in Blenheim yesterday. She'd spent hours trawling through shops, trying to decide on gifts for the most important males in her life.

'Hell, no. It was part of the ritual. Drove Mum crazy. I think she expected me to break something.'

'One year Mum wrapped up books, loads of them, and put them under the tree. We really believed that was what we were getting—books.' Mum. She'd have these same memories, too.

Cam must've heard her sigh because his arm wound around her shoulders and tugged her close to his strong body. 'It's not too late to ask your parents to join my family at the farm for Christmas.'

Twisting awkwardly, she stared up into the face she loved. 'Really? Would your mother mind? She already has a house full coming that day.'

He squeezed her gently. 'She'd love it. So would Dad. They can't wait to meet you, by the way.' He'd phoned them earlier in the day and she'd heard him laughing and chatting so easily. Seemed he had a great relationship with his family.

As did she, Jenny acknowledged. When she'd

arrived at home last week they'd opened their arms and hugged her like it had been only the day before she'd left Dunedin. 'I'll phone them now.'

'Don't talk all night. I'm looking forward to going to bed.'

The last time this gorgeous man had mentioned going to bed she'd imagined what it might be like. Now, after their lovemaking in Kahurangi and over the last two nights, she had a few clues. 'Maybe I'm worth waiting for.' She grinned.

'Lady, I waited a whole week to make love to you again. That was more than enough.'

Thank goodness Dad answered her call. He disliked talking on the phone so the conversation was brief and successful. 'Dad will email me flight details tomorrow.' Jenny dropped her phone on the table and took Cam's hand. 'Come on. What are you sitting around here for?'

Cam stood up and reached for her. When his lips brushed her mouth she all but melted. 'Bedroom. Fast.'

The next morning she was woken by the twins bringing her a cup of tea. 'Thanks, Andrew,

Marcus.' She stretched her toes towards the end of the king-size bed. 'I definitely could get used to this,' she said, repeating what she'd said the first morning she'd woken up in this house. Though that had been in the bedroom down the hall.

'Have you seen all the presents under the tree?' Andrew asked.

'There are lots and lots and lots.' Marcus grinned.

'It's exciting, isn't it?' She grinned back. 'Where's your dad?'

'Getting breakfast.'

'We're having a barbecue.'

'Bacon and eggs.'

'And hash browns and mushrooms.'

Jenny's head was spinning as the boys gabbled at her. 'I'd better get up, then. I don't want to miss out.'

'Finish your tea first.' Cam stood in the doorway, looking at her with love in his eyes. 'We've got all morning.'

She shook her head at him. 'I've got to go to the grocery store later. We're going to make double chocolate chip Santa biscuits this morning.'

* * *

The kitchen turned into a familiar mess as Jenny supervised the mixing of the biscuit batter. 'How does flour spread so far?' she mock growled at the boys.

'Something to do with the way you shake the packet as you're filling the measuring cup,' Cam said. 'I've never seen anyone create flour clouds before.'

'Hey!' Jenny caught Marcus's hand before it reached his mouth. 'Don't eat all those chocolate buttons. We need some for the cookies.'

Andrew quickly shovelled a handful into his mouth and began chewing hard. His eyes bulged as he tried not to laugh.

'Not fair,' Marcus grumped.

Jenny let go his hand and reached into the shopping bag. 'Just as well I bought double the quantity needed.'

'You're spoiling them.' Cam helped himself to a few buttons. Then he picked up some more and began feeding her one by one.

Her tongue grazed his fingertips and she saw the jolt of hot need zipping through his eyes, felt the reciprocal desire heat her body.

In the background she thought she heard 'Yuck' and 'Gross' but she couldn't be sure and she wasn't stopping to ask the boys what they'd said. Then reality slipped into the heat haze that was her mind right now. The boys. They weren't alone. She pulled away.

'Welcome to the real world,' Cam whispered.

Funny how that only made her feel happier. 'Better get these cookies in the oven. Marcus, can you cut the Santa shapes while, Andrew, you can put the liquorice on their chins.'

Cam shook his head. 'Talk about left-field Santas.'

The boys hurried through their tasks and then went over to the tree to rustle amongst the parcels.

'Hey, guys, leave those for Christmas Day.' Cam spoke firmly.

'We're giving Jenny ours now.'

'Are you sure you don't want to wait?' Cam wore a frown.

'She needs it as soon as possible.'

What's going on? Jenny looked from Cam to his sons and back. 'I can wait.'

'No, you can't,' Andrew informed her, as he

lifted a square parcel from the back of all the presents.

'We want you to have this.' Marcus took a corner of the present.

Together the boys handed it over to her. 'We made it.'

Jenny took the proffered gift. 'Thank you, Andrew. Thank you, Marcus.' She dropped a kiss on each forehead before glancing up at Cam to see him swallowing hard. *What was this?*

It felt hard and flat-sided, and she very carefully unwrapped the parcel. As the red and green paper fell aside she found a wooden box with a tiny bronze lock and key and it was painted bright green. 'You made this?' she asked around the tears in her throat. 'For me? It's beautiful.'

'It's to put your mojo in.'

'We don't want you to lose it again.'

The floor pushed up at the bottoms of her feet. She grabbed the counter to remain upright, holding on until the dizziness abated. 'Thank you,' she managed to whisper, before the floodgates opened and the tears became a torrent. Running a hand over the box, she twisted the key and lifted the lid. 'Thank you,' she repeated.

Cam's hand was warm on her shoulder. 'You okay?'

'More than okay. You have the world's best two boys.'

'I reckon.'

Marcus said, 'We're glad we found you in the shop.'

'Jenny,' Andrew said. 'Are you going to the farm with us for Christmas?'

'Yes. Your dad asked me last night.' Between kisses.

'Are you staying for ever?'

Jenny raised her gaze to Cam's, gave him a watery smile. 'I hope so.'

One of the boys—she wasn't sure which for all the hammering of her heart echoing in her head—asked, 'Can we have a wedding? Like Toby Sorenson's parents did? That was cool.'

Cam grinned. 'That's meant to be my line, guys.'

Jenny was speechless. Her eyes took in Cam and Marcus and Andrew all staring at her, waiting for something from her. Her mouth dropped open but no words came out. Deep inside the final knot in her stomach unravelled, spreading warmth and love through her. Her chest rose as she drew in a breath. 'Yes, let's have a wedding.'

'Cool.'

'Cool.'

Cam said, 'I love you.'

'And I love the three of you.' Another flood of tears began. Talk about getting all her Christmases in one year.

Impervious to the tears, Cam reached for her and kissed her, long and lovingly. 'I love you,' he whispered again, and went back to kissing her.

And for once the boys refrained from saying a word. Jenny knew that thankfully it was only a respite, not a permanent change. She loved her family just the way they were.

As Cam finally lifted his mouth from those delectable lips he smiled like the cat with the cream.

Note to self: never let a day go by without remembering how much you love this woman.

* * * * *

MILLS & BOON®
Large Print Medical

July

August

September

MILLS & BOON®
Large Print Medical

October

JUST ONE NIGHT?	Carol Marinelli
MEANT-TO-BE FAMILY	Marion Lennox
THE SOLDIER SHE COULD NEVER FORGET	Tina Beckett
THE DOCTOR'S REDEMPTION	Susan Carlisle
WANTED: PARENTS FOR A BABY!	Laura Iding
HIS PERFECT BRIDE?	Louisa Heaton

November

ALWAYS THE MIDWIFE	Alison Roberts
MIDWIFE'S BABY BUMP	Susanne Hampton
A KISS TO MELT HER HEART	Emily Forbes
TEMPTED BY HER ITALIAN SURGEON	Louisa George
DARING TO DATE HER EX	Annie Claydon
THE ONE MAN TO HEAL HER	Meredith Webber

December

MIDWIFE...TO MUM!	Sue MacKay
HIS BEST FRIEND'S BABY	Susan Carlisle
ITALIAN SURGEON TO THE STARS	Melanie Milburne
HER GREEK DOCTOR'S PROPOSAL	Robin Gianna
NEW YORK DOC TO BLUSHING BRIDE	Janice Lynn
STILL MARRIED TO HER EX!	Lucy Clark

0615 LP 2P P2 Medi